Middle-Aged
Boys & Girls

Essential Prose Series 126

Canada Council **Conseil des Arts**
for the Arts **du Canada**

ONTARIO ARTS COUNCIL
CONSEIL DES ARTS DE L'ONTARIO
an Ontario government agency
un organisme du gouvernement de l'Ontario

Canadä

Guernica Editions Inc. acknowledges the support of the Canada Council
for the Arts and the Ontario Arts Council. The Ontario Arts Council
is an agency of the Government of Ontario.

We acknowledge the financial support of the Government of Canada.
Nous reconnaissons l'appui financier du gouvernement du Canada.

Middle-Aged Boys & Girls

Diane Bracuk

GUERNICA
EDITIONS
TORONTO • BUFFALO • LANCASTER (U.K.)
2016

Michael Mirolla, general editor
Ged Stankus, cover design
Dennis Wojda, cover illustration
David Moratto, interior design
Guernica Editions Inc.
1569 Heritage Way, Oakville, (ON), Canada L6M 2Z7
2250 Military Road, Tonawanda, N.Y. 14150-6000 U.S.A.
www.guernicaeditions.com

Distributors:
University of Toronto Press Distribution,
5201 Dufferin Street, Toronto (ON), Canada M3H 5T8
Gazelle Book Services, White Cross Mills, High Town,
Lancaster LA1 4XS U.K.

First edition.
Printed in Canada.

Legal Deposit—First Quarter
Library of Congress Catalog Card Number: 2015949360
Library and Archives Canada Cataloguing in Publication
Bracuk, Diane, 1955-, author
Middle-aged boys & girls / Diane Bracuk. —First edition.

(Essential prose series ; 126)
Short stories.
Issued in print and electronic formats.
ISBN 978-1-77183-069-0 (paperback).--ISBN 978-1-77183-070-6
(epub).--ISBN 978-1-77183-071-3 (mobi)

I. Title. II. Title: Middle-aged boys and girls.
III. Series: Essential prose series ; 126

PS8603.R3266M54 2016   C813'.6   C2015-905887-2   C2015-905888-0

Contents

Shadow Selves

You were naked a lot in those days. Or *nude*, you liked to put it, rolling out the word in your purring way, basking in the indecency of it, your ability to shock. A two-hundred-pound woman clothed is one thing. But to see that woman bare, so flagrantly undressed, breasts falling full down to her waist, stomach sharply folding ...

We lived in a low rise in Toronto's Annex, three floors apart. Even in the middle of winter when I came down to see you, you would be *nude*. Or scantily clad, engrossed in some ordinary task like painting your perfectly pedicured toenails, or just puttering about. You were very aware that your *curves*, as you called them, were on display. Flaunted to maximum effect in your *boudoir*: lavender walls, plump sofas, antique brocade cushions. Reclining, you reminded me of an odalisque by Rubens, a celebration of lustrous skin tones. Or a Renoir, impressionistic dapplings of flesh so light-filled as to seem lightweight. Yet for all your languor, I read something defiant in your face. Challenging me—or anyone—to dispute that your size, so celebrated in another century, still wasn't desirable.

It was the early '80s, a decade before the first magazines for full-figured women would appear with their mandate that attractiveness shouldn't be dictated by dress size. "Is she crazy?" would sometimes flutter to my mind. But I was a newcomer to the big city, and you were my closest confidante. Censoring critical thoughts about you had become second nature.

* * *

There is a psychological theory that holds that who we believe ourselves to be is chiefly defined in terms of what we are not. When we are drawn to someone markedly different from ourselves, that difference represents our repressed or "shadow" self: the one we need to develop for personal growth.

I was slim, but pear-shaped. Or bulbous, I thought, seeing my shape more aligned with hoary root vegetables than sweet-tasting fruit. While you seemingly loved your body, I loathed mine; the imperfections of my proportions always looming in front of me, the bulk in one place, the meagreness in another. A defect my high cheekbones did little to assuage. If you were the odalisque of art, then I was the grim Eve in a Gothic altarpiece. Swollen hips, small breasts. Body huddled, as if cowering in shame at being cast out from an Eden of physical perfection.

Although fascinated by your ability to enjoy your body, I couldn't condone it. Inherent in our friendship was an unspoken assumption that you would lose weight. You never mentioned your weight except to say that on a metaphysical level your flesh served to protect you from being overwhelmed by men, that dam-burst of attention that would inevitably deluge you if you were slim. Somehow I believed this; believed your weight would come off when you were ready. No banal diets or treadmills for you. I imagined you slipping out of your excess flesh as if it were a quilted jumpsuit.

"You'll be so beautiful then," I once said.

And you shot back: "I'm already beautiful."

We were twenty-eight and single. "Getting on," if we were being judged by conventional standards, which we vehemently refused to accept. Our common bond was that we were both late bloomers. Overcomers of great psychological obstacles. We had both moved to Toronto three years earlier in rebellion against our upbringings. Mine was rural western, Polish peasant mentality: don't expect much out of life. Yours, Montreal JAP: demand *all*.

I was a copywriter at an ad agency. You were a receptionist at a ticket office, a job that was beneath you. But you professed more interest in your "inner work". We spoke about that a lot, the "inner work" that we still needed to do. Dealing with our anger. Sadness. The hard-done-by inner child that precluded us from even considering having kids of our own. Hermetically sealed in self-absorption, we consulted therapists, psychics, and the stars. "Not being ready" for a relationship exempted us from the marriage anxiety of other women our age. If our love lives weren't progressing as they should, it was simply because we couldn't handle anymore just now.

I still take refuge in that philosophy. Use it as an excuse for not having organized the ten—or can it be closer to twenty?—years of notes behind this essay, which originally started out as a letter of apology. All I've written today is one paragraph, a puny accomplishment that I bask in, telling myself it's all I was ready for. No admission of procrastination. I didn't fail, I just fell short of an ill-defined goal. But, as you must have feared, I now surround myself with mirror images of myself—slim, focused women who see my lulls for what they are, and who urge me to "get on with it."

* * *

It was a Saturday; we were in your apartment reading. Consulting the *Cosmopolitan* "Love Scope for Men," which I'd half-jokingly bought for advice. A lawyer I had met through work had asked me out for dinner that night. Jim Park. A posh WASP name that went with his flawless patrician looks, turning my mind into a pinball machine of ricocheting anxieties that it was your role to appease.

Soft sunlight poured through your living room window, making the lavender walls look more flesh-toned. You too had a date that evening, a romantic dinner for two, for which you had been making elaborate preparations since early morning. Sheer lace doilies draped the lampshades. An embroidered linen tablecloth that you had steamed, damp rolled, and then ironed adorned the dining room table. Over your sofa was a collection of Japanese fans, which you had artfully rearranged; next to that, a vase of fresh cut flowers. Although our apartments were small, yours seemed commodious, as if the ceiling were domed like a marbleized Turkish bath.

As usual, you looked as if you had just stepped out of one, wrapped in a huge silk scarf that knotted above your breasts. The fabric looked as if it were cut from a tropical flower, the coral-red shade supersaturated as if sap were still running through it. You were in the kitchen making sushi appetizers for dinner. Dainty, unfattening bits of avocado and crabmeat rolled into fragrant sticky rice. ("Did she pig out a lot?" another friend once asked me. "Never in front of me," I answered.) The mingled smells of rice and damp linen permeated the room with a moist, talcum-y freshness that almost felt maternal.

I glanced at the obligatory sultry model on the *Cosmo* cover, and flipped to the table of contents. "How to make him wild in bed. How to tell if he'll commit. How to tell if he's having an affair. How to blast your butt for bikini season. What? No Plato?"

You laughed at my frail humour, tilting your head back into an exaggerated guffaw. I luxuriated in your laugh. It was like no other: lush, mellifluous, rolling along deeply guttered valleys or whipping up into peaks of shrieking hilarity. To my silliest remarks, you supplied what sounded like a standing ovation. It was the balm I needed.

Despite my neuroses, I was, for the first time in my life, popular with men. Upscale, exclusive men whom I met through my advertising friends; men of a type who, in my former mid-western isolation, had not even existed for me.

You too had men, but they were not my idea of men to date. No job, no money, but doing a lot of "inner work" too, to redress that negative balance. Your longest relationship had been with an Algerian waiter from Paris (later you ruefully admitted he was trying to obtain a visa). When you mentioned "your men," I generally tuned out. Made perfunctory remarks, then shuttled back to my life, my problems.

"And now, 'The Astrological Guide to Pleasing the Man in Your Life,'" I said in a mocking tone. "OK. Jim's a Taurus. You're a Taurus. Taurus people are very sensual, right?"

You reached to get a plate out of your cupboard, exposing a glimpse of pubic hair as the scarf parted at your thighs. "We Taureans are *very* sensual," you said.

"He likes candlelight, fine dining and ... if you really want to turn him on, skinny dipping in the moonlight," I read.

Your voice caught in a small gasp of longing. "Oh, that's me! I love skinny dipping in the moonlight!"

"Well, he has a cottage in Muskoka that he goes to every summer ... So I guess if I'm still going out with him then ..."

"Invite me."

But I had set the magazine down, shoulders already contracting in their Gothic hunch, wanting to cover myself up. Summer, the season of bathing suits, had always been a time of heightened neurotic scrutiny for me. I could already see myself at Jim's cottage. The escarpment. Blue water. His physically perfect prep school friends. Me, taking it in in furtive snatches, too consumed with what my behind looked like from any given angle to relax.

Then there was you, with your ... weight; so comfortable, so at ease with yourself. Today your size looked minimized, and I could see why you said men loved your curves. (Again, with that slight edge of defiance as if challenging someone—me?—to tell you it wasn't true.) But at this moment it was. With the moisture in the air from ironing and cooking, your body looked smoother, steamed at the joints into more pliable softness. It seemed unfair that I was being asked out to the nicer places, for I could see you in a moonlit pool, offering up your warm wet body as something fragrant and delicious.

You placed a coin of sushi in front of me to sample. Ignoring it, I flipped, not joking anymore, to the article called "Ten Ways to Blast your Butt."

"Well, this will bring me up to a grand total of knowing eight thousand ways to blast my butt. And as far as I can tell, none of them work."

An old quip you'd heard too many times, which was really a plea for reassurance. Nevertheless, your laughter roller-coastered around the room and, after a sombre pause, you told me I looked just fine.

* * *

The next morning we commiserated about our respective dates. Mine was my usual regurgitation of every witticism I hoped I'd made (ho, ho, ho, you chortled on cue); yours less cerebral. For dinner, you had worn a white silk kimono, *nude* underneath, and oh, I should have seen Enrico's face when you answered the door. As with all men, he couldn't keep his hands off you, and within minutes of entering your apartment, the kimono was off.

"Then we lay for a long while on the floor kissing each other's stomachs. I found that so emotional ... so romantic ... I almost cried."

I looked down at my stomach, bloated from last night's dinner at a French restaurant. Atonement, in the form of a five-mile run, up and down the hills around Avenue Road, was coming up. Jim had also intimated that he might invite me to his cottage, and mentally I was barricading my freezer compartment with brick-like boxes of Lean Cuisine.

"It sounds a little lewd," I said off-handedly.

You chuckled a low, lascivious laugh. "Oh, it was absolutely *obscene*. Especially when he started to eat off me."

My head jerked up. "He *ate* off you?"

"Uh huh. He said my skin tasted so good that he wanted to lick food off it. So we put the sushi on my stomach and he ate them off me."

"He *ate* off you?"

"Uh huh." You scrunched your shoulders in rapturous delight, savouring the memory and its shock value. "Oh! And we had truffles for dessert! And I hid them in a secret place somewhere! Guess where?"

Your voice was coy and breathless. I looked around your apartment, at your kitchen, your sofa, your table, which despite being so beautifully set, apparently hadn't been used after all. "In your cupboards?"

"Nooo ..."

"In your bedroom?"

"Nooo ..."

"That vase?"

"Nooo ... someplace more intimate than that."

"On your body?" I paused: recoiled. "*In* your body?"

"He had to find them with his tongue!" A whoop of laughter broke loose and somersaulted around the room. "Oh look at your face! Just look at your face! You are such a prude! I can't believe you sometimes!"

* * *

I read somewhere that we should try to be on nodding terms with the people we used to be whether we find them attractive or not. Confronted with my 28-year-old self, I want to cross the street to get away from her, like a child with eccentric parents. But if there is absolution in making these grudging reconnections (and I believe I am writing this partially as a bid for absolution from what came next), then I join my former self around your dining room table.

* * *

It was a cold, rainy day in late October, and there was no comfort in your place, for it had undergone a radical transformation. Your psychic had said you could raise your vibrational level by changing your décor, which you had done with unnerving vigour, repainting the pastel walls a livid-looking rooster red and replacing your linen tablecloth with one patterned in swirls of colliding colours. From the kitchen came the pungent, slightly yeasty smell of an herbal concoction you were brewing to clear the air of negative energy. Underlying that was a heavier, familiar, greasy smell, which I couldn't identify.

You sat across from me, wrapped in a hot pink floral muumuu, your face flushed. My immediate thought, which I pushed away, was that you looked bigger. Obdurate somehow. Your limbs not light, but like waterlogged sandbags, thighs spread over the chair as if taking possession of it. It occurred to me that this was the first time I had ever allowed myself to see your flesh as real, rather than rendered in the tints and glazes of an Old Master.

"I haven't seen you for a while," you said, an edge of accusation in your voice.

"Oh, I know. But it's been so busy at the agency lately. A ton of campaigns. After-work functions."

You sat in disapproving silence, your eyes glazed and

stony. To your way of thinking, I was doing much too much with my advertising friends. Running myself ragged with superficial socializing, not taking enough time for our all-important "inner work."

I began fidgeting with the tablecloth, noting how snake-like the swirls were, tails joined to mouth in a vicious circle. It was true. I had withdrawn from you lately. But it wasn't because of work. A recent disappointment had hit me harder than I thought it would, and it now pained me to have to bring it up.

"Well, I'll probably have more time now. I'm not seeing Jim anymore," I said. Then added quickly: "It was mutual. We both decided something was missing, and that we're better off being good friends."

You crossed one leg, flashing me the obligatory glimpse of pubic hair. Then in a distant, semi-mystical voice you said that you too had ended a relationship—your relationship with Enrico. He had phoned one day requesting "a little afternoon delight," and when you told him no, he said: "Come on, baby." You hung up on him then, which you had never done with a man before, a significant emotional shift according to your therapist.

But I was barely listening. All I could think about was that my relationship with Jim had only lasted three months. Like the one before that, and the one before that. Three years of three-month relationships, a pattern set—and congealing.

"Of course, I knew from the start that we weren't compatible," I said, rushing on. "He probably needs someone more earthy than I am. A spontaneous, skinny-dipping type."

"I agree," you said bluntly.

"In fact, I was thinking of setting him up with someone at work. Alix, the new account person." My classic defence mechanism at the time—showing how indifferent I was to rejection by setting my ex-boyfriend up with someone else.

You drew yourself up straighter and squared your shoulders.

"Set him up with me," you said.

"Pardon?"

"Set him up with me."

"You?"

"From everything you've told me about him, I know I'm his type."

I looked at your face, which in the past two minutes seemed to have become heavier. A line, an interior social boundary between us, which I thought you had always acknowledged and accepted, had been crossed. Your flesh, which now looked like an imposing mass, emitted a dank, off-putting odour of musk and thwarted lust. A moment of truth hung before us, and I was overcome by the revulsion that had always run latent beneath my admiration for you.

"Jim likes fit women," I said evenly.

"I'm very fit," you said.

"Skinny, then. Model-like. *Thin.*"

You sat erect, your face a mask of sullen implacability. The topic had to be closed fast. But a perverse streak in me almost wanted you to continue arguing your conviction that you were Jim's type. You could actually see yourself with him? Flaunting your big, bovine body? Around his perfect, snobby, patrician friends? What did that say about you? Worse, what did it say about me, being drawn to someone so self-deluded? A horrible vision of the future flashed before me. The two of us at 50, spinsters, still living in this building, my place becoming shabbier, yours belligerently brighter as dictated by psychics. And you still parading around *nude*, steely grey pubic hair bristling between your thunder thighs like cut electrical wires.

I grasped at our old standby. "You probably aren't ready for a relationship."

You nodded, hostility momentarily replaced by a sad acceptance. "Neither of us is," you said.

I looked away, trying to shrug that one off. Your place seemed to be closing in on me, the walls swelling from the intermingled smells. Mumbling something about having to prepare for a big presentation the next morning, I rose from my chair.

"When are we going to get together again?" you asked.

"I don't know. Like I said, we've been really busy at the agency."

"Shall we set a date for Sunday?"

The word date set off new alarm bells in my head. A lifetime of dating one another. Our dates with the opposite sex becoming increasingly uncertain, but with each other a depressing given.

"All right, but I can't promise."

I wanted to leave. For good, I suddenly realized. Get the hell out of there and never come back. But I remained rooted in your kitchen, racked by guilt and a sense of ethical wrong-doing. Female friendships, especially those defined by fuzzy feminist ideals, are supposed to be nobler, not so easily discarded. I needed some excuse, the proverbial last straw that would cleanse me of any ambivalence. The underlying smell rose in my nostrils, now gloatingly identifiable.

"Have you been eating French fries?" I asked.

You paused for a long moment, then said matter-of-factly: "I fried up a whole bag of them before you came here. I had a craving for carbohydrates."

"A *whole* bag?"

You nodded unrepentantly.

My voice became prissy with reprimand, outraged by your candour, which could only force a crueler honesty on my part. "If you were craving carbohydrates, couldn't you have boiled up some potatoes, and eaten them without butter?"

Your expression was closed, but for a second I saw a bitter, mirthful glint in your eyes, as if you wanted to burst out laughing at my earnestness.

"I couldn't resist," you said flatly.

* * *

We both believed that, when we were truly ready for something, the universe would provide. And so, when a work colleague told me about an apartment that had become vacant in a fashionable, downtown high-rise, I found myself, within a month, living airborne on the 18th floor, with people I'd never know in the apartments below me. A huge picture window in my living room looked out onto a white winter sky. I planned my next incarnation on this blank slate, a new self, untouched by shadows.

Yet I still am. To say I'm "haunted" by your memory is too romantic and self-serving in the way it circumvents my callow abandonment of you (made all the easier by your dignified refusal not to fight for our friendship: "You phone me," was all you said when I began cancelling our dates).

But my fascination with women who dare to be bigger than society's norm has never gone away.

There are least two magazines devoted to big, bold, and beautiful women. I flip through them at the convenience store while buying last-minute things for dinner, compulsively checking the fat content of food (while telling myself it's because of my husband's cholesterol). These magazines have upbeat editorials, grateful letters to the editor, and lovely large women (although rarely as large as yourself) modelling bathing suits, tight jeans, and wedding dresses. Many are in slinky lingerie, saucily provocative, as they should be. But never the full reveal of abundant, bare flesh.

Art historian Kenneth Clarke has said that the English language distinguishes between the naked and the nude: "To be naked is to be deprived of clothes, and feel the embarrassment most of us feel in that condition. The word nude, on the other hand, carries an educated usage, no uncomfortable undertones. The image it projects is not of a huddled and defenceless body, but of a balanced, prosperous, and confident body, the body reformed."

When I think of you now, it is in full-blown heroic terms, an aesthetic reformer who refused to bow to society's dictates. And I wish the best for you, that some man you love is "kissing and kissing" your stomach. Or showing you off at a French restaurant, which is probably what you would prefer. I wonder though, were you truly nude? Your compulsive exhibitionism forced me to confront not only who I was, but who you were, too. Look at me, this me, accept all of me, every square inch of me, you proclaimed. Such naked need. Such naked desire. How could I not run?

Prey

From the moment she arrived at the train station, Sandra knew that she should have taken the plane to Riga. The sudden stop, the surly porter, then, as she stepped down on the platform, the familiar projectile of pain piercing her left thigh. Ahead were the cliff-like, Soviet-era steps she would now have to navigate with her throbbing leg and roll-on luggage. Planting her right foot firmly on the first step she began her graceless choreography—one step, luggage up, leg up, breath caught to absorb the fresh jabs of pain—then finally she was on the sidewalk, which was awash in harsh sunlight.

In Sopot, the jewel of the Baltic Sea, where she had spent the last three days, there had been cabs everywhere. Only one car was on this street, a beat-up old Volkswagen with a round-faced, blond man slumped at the wheel.

She rapped at the window. "Taxi? Taxi?"

He opened his eyes, a bloodshot and startled blue that reminded her of Curly in "The Three Stooges."

"Hotel," she said, pointing to the picture of the B&B in the brochure she was clutching. "*Hotel.* Do you know where it is?"

He scampered out to get her luggage. "Jah, jah."

She had barely squeezed herself into the back seat when he was off, hurtling toward a stretch of grey Soviet apartment blocks, which looked as if they had formed from some ominous cloudbank that had rolled over the Baltic Sea. Amplifying their ugliness was graffiti, what looked like Polish swear words, huge, prickly thickets of letters whooshing by until the cab lurched to a stop in front of a building emblazoned with a simple "FUC U."

"Hotel," he said, pointing to the town square.

"Which one is it?"

He jabbed his finger into space. "*Here!*"

At least the buildings in the square looked similar to the ones in the brochure that she had used to make her reservation earlier that morning with Lucazs, the handsome young concierge at her Sopot hotel who had been so pleased to practice his English with her.

She spotted a café sign. "OK, I'll find it then. No, thank you very much. I can take my own luggage. No, that's OK. I'm *fine.*"

She was in an empty square of closely packed, tall, narrow houses. Hundreds of towns like this had been built all along the Baltic coastline, from the days when this part of Poland, with its much-sought-after amber, was part of the prosperous, Dutch-ruled Hanseatic Trading League. Already she could see by the more constricted-looking places around her that it wouldn't be quite what she was used to in Sopot, but that was the point of taking the train trip, wasn't it? Seeing the *real* Poland, the part of the country from where her grandmother came versus her brand of bubble tourism. In Sopot she had enjoyed a creamed herring dish—wonderfully delicate, nothing like her Uncle Stanislaw's stinky, pickled concoctions—and hoped she could get one of at least a similar quality at the café here while she got her bearings. Lugging her leg and luggage over the uneven cobblestones, she plopped herself on a chair beside a rusting metal table.

"Arthritis," her doctor had said, but she referred to it more romantically as her *affliction*.

"Just my affliction," she'd say when friends started pointing out her limp. "Had to give up pole dancing."

Pain was too inadequate a word to describe the flare-ups that came and went. It was as if a sodden log of driftwood had been rammed up her hip joint, splintering it into fragments, and pulling her off balance. Once she got to her room, she'd rest, read, and perhaps try her new amber cream, which was touted to contain a natural healer: fossilized tree resin.

She shoved her luggage under the table. Right now she needed to down one of Big Pharma's healers, her pain meds, with a glass of water. Why wasn't anyone in the café coming out to serve her? And where were all the people? This wasn't like southern countries where people took siestas.

She decided to text her friend in Riga, slipping her BlackBerry out of her purse: "Looks like customer service has yet to arrive in this part of Poland." But, nothing. Just a smudgy black rectangle staring back at her, even though it had worked perfectly that morning.

A woman emerged from the café; old, stocky, clumping toward her in a shapeless navy coat and a pair of mannish, lace-up shoes.

"Hotel?" she asked, stone-faced.

Sandra tried not to stare at her hair, an enormous, messy grey bun, almost aggressively unstylish, as if a dusty hornet's nest had been pinned on top of her head.

"No, thank you. I already have a room," she said politely. "Could I have some water please?" She made the shape of a bottle with her hands, and then, in the same improvised sign language, a drinking motion. "Bottled water, please? No gas."

The woman looked confused for a second, then blurted. "Not here."

"*What* not here? No water here?"

She pointed to the café. "Tat. Here!"

It had always struck Sandra how harsh and guttural Polish, the language she had grown up with but had never wanted to learn, could sound when spoken in anger. "People from the dark ages," Lucazs had explained when Sandra inquired about the rudeness of some of the service people, who stubbornly refused to answer even the simplest questions. "They want things back the way they were before."

"Oh, I get it. You want me to go inside." Standing up, Sandra felt a sickening click in her joint, as if her leg might suddenly snap off. Instantly she sat down.

"No. *Here!*"

"I heard you, OK? I'll go inside, to *there*, but I need a bit of help. If you could just help me with my bag ..."

The woman nodded and leaned closer to fetch her luggage, looking animated for the first time. Or was it sly? Sandra's hand went up, stopping the woman.

"No. I've changed my mind. I'm not going there. I'm staying *here*."

* * *

When I was filling out the customer service form under Lucazs' cool green gaze, so much like yours, but not mocking, I wanted to write "thanks for not flirting with me to get a good review. Thanks for not playing me like some gullible old cougar, grateful for every crumb of attention."

"You're either prey or predator," you had told me on our first date.

We had been talking about Poland, to which I was making my second visit, about its history as a damaged, defeated nation, which had the misfortune to be sandwiched between Germany and Russia. I was taken aback, not just by your juvenile political perspective, but by the way you said it, boldly locking eyes with me. In those days, I didn't have my affliction, so I excused myself to go to the ladies' room, sassily showing off what was then a still shapely behind. Reapplying my lipstick, I tried to absorb your harrowing life story. Running away from your abusive mother at 16, being homeless, living off various women, until you became a father.

"Prey or predator! Well, that's very interesting. What are you?" I asked when I got back to the table, noticing that you had ordered another round of drinks.

"It all depends," you grinned ambiguously.

"I don't think I'm either. Maybe I started out as prey, with low self-esteem. It was the way I was raised by my immigrant parents: 'Can't do this, don't try that.' But I was determined to overcome that."

"I could tell that by your photo. I thought: Now that's one smart woman, who knows what she's doing. I didn't even know whether I should try to contact you because I knew other guys would be hitting on you."

I nodded, keeping my expression sphinx-like. In fact, I

had been shocked by how few responses I got on my first attempt at online dating, something I thought I would have been prepared for at my age. When I was ready to give up, your face popped up on my profile, eyes tilted like those of a baby fox.

"To go back to your story, the homeless part," I said.

"Look, I'm not Biff from the country club, like your ex-husband. I couldn't exactly dip into my trust fund."

"Well, I'm not exactly tight with my old country club crowd anymore now that I'm divorced. I think they find my new passion for my Polish roots to be embarrassing. At the last dinner party I was invited to, a good friend said: 'Oh Sandra, *must* you talk about all those *depressing* Polish books?'"

"Right. Versus the funny ones about the death camps," you said.

"Or those hysterical ones about the Stalinist era."

"Those deportations to Siberia? They always crack me up."

"Look, they're snobs," I said. "Always were, always will be. I'm going from my Gatsby stage to my Gatski stage, and they don't like it."

We exchanged torrid glances.

"Maybe the wives are jealous of you," you said.

"Why would they be jealous of me?"

"The rich divorcee, who's still got it."

How I preened at that, shamefully so in memory for, while I would have been put off by you calling me "hot" or a "babe" at my age, still having "it"—the illusive "it" factor that transcended looks or age, was plausible.

"Let's get back to your living on the street, then living off women. Playing them."

You frowned, and looked down. "I have a daughter now. It's not something I'm proud of."

"Sorry. I'm not trying to make you feel bad. I'm impressed that you went into social work and turned your life around."

A drink later, I leaned in closer, our faces almost touching.

"So tell me," I said. "Is this something you put on your resume? *Confidence* man?"

* * *

Which of these places was her B&B, she wondered again, squinting across the square. That house directly across from her, the same blood red as the one in the brochure, or its more rusty toned neighbour? Had she not been worried that her leg, now throbbing like an abscessed tooth, would give out on her, she would hobble over, and knock on doors until she found it.

On the train here, she had read another depressing book on Poland, about the decades of unrelenting fear in this area. Nazis shooting whole villages, the Red Army dragging off survivors in the middle of the night and, most recently, just under 20 years ago, martial law.

And now, in the middle of the day, it was as if another massive evacuation had taken place, the tiny black rectangles of windows staring blankly at her. How strange that she hadn't seen a single soul, not even a car in what should be a bustling town square. Was there a factory outside where everyone worked? A relic from the dark days, pumping out shoddy goods, situated miles away from town since mind-numbing inconvenience had also been part of the Communist creed?

If her BlackBerry were working, she'd phone Lucazs.

"Excellent," she had rated him on the customer service form that was so new to Poland, adding in the comment section that he had "gone the extra mile for her." Seeing his puzzled expression, she explained: "It means going out of your way to serve people."

Paint apparently was also in short supply during Soviet rule, so these houses, so faithfully reproduced in their bright Hanseatic League colours, must have been, until recently, depressingly dingy. Yet there's something off about them, she thought, glancing compulsively at another window. Almost begrudgingly bright, as if the paint had been slapped on in order to align them with the edicts of capitalism and a tourist trade for which they had never asked.

A wizened face flickered at one of the windows, then disappeared.

The first pulse of panic went through her. These homes were not empty after all. People were in them, watching her. Probably from the time she had limped into the square, waving away the café owner, who, an unwelcome suspicion was telling her, could very well be the town thief.

Drawing her dead BlackBerry closer to her chest, she pretended to type out a chirpy message to her friend in Riga. *Hi there! Just sitting around waiting to be mugged! Affliction flared up, so can't walk away, much less run!* Out of the corner of her eye, she saw the woman approaching her again from the café, followed by a stout, blond man. Curly, her cab driver?

* * *

After our first Match.com date, I prepared dozens of polite reasons why we couldn't get together again. But it didn't matter, because you didn't get back to me. I had almost forgotten about you when an email popped up one Friday night, asking if I was still having that torrid affair with Brad from the country club and, if not, would I care to join you for a drink?

"So tell me, when you were out on the street scoping out a woman for your next meal ticket, who would you pick?"

We were having drinks at an outdoor patio downtown, a regular haunt for what was turning out to be our occasional, last-minute get-togethers—which suited me, because I didn't want to be in a closer relationship with you. Just a playmate, not a keeper, I thought, nevertheless getting girlishly excited whenever one of your messages would appear. *Hey Veronica! Want to go out for a soda pop? Archie. Hey Jackie! Want to see my new yacht? Ari.*

You took a sip of your wine, and sucked in your cheeks with an air of injured dignity.

"That was a long time ago and my daughter has made me a totally different person. I really don't like to talk about those days."

"Oh, I understand. I'm not trying to make you feel bad. But just humour me, OK? I'm curious to see what kind of woman a con man would prey on, that's all. Wait! Let's see if I can figure it out!"

This particular bar had been a favourite watering hole of my old advertising crowd in the '90s, and many of its regulars were middle-aged hipsters. I pointed to an attractive woman around my age, wearing a casually chic vest and pants, her brown hair pulled back in a classic ponytail.

"That one?"

"Could you be a little more discreet?"

"I am! Just answer me. Would you have tried to hustle her?"

You studied her with your cool jade eyes, with lashes longer and thicker than anything I could have ever have achieved with even two coats of mascara. When you were a boy, you said, your mother made you do your own laundry, and I thought how could any mother look into those eyes gazing at her over an ironing board and not melt?

"Nah. She'd be too smart to buy my story."

At the table next to us were three women who I had mentally labelled the Paris Hilton wannabes, with their blonde hair, bling, and mammoth designer purses.

"What about her?" I asked, indicating the oldest of the bunch, whose lips were pinched by deep, bitter lines.

You shrugged.

Her companion, chubby and buxom in a low-cut tank dress, was fussing with an unhappy looking toy Chihuahua in her purse, lamenting about the time he had once peed in her lap.

"Her?"

Looking embarrassed, but resolute, as if it took a certain courage to own up to something, you paused, then nodded. "Yes. Someone like her could have possibly been a candidate."

A good con, you said hours later, after we had ordered drinks for last call, has to contain a mix of lies and truth, a plausible reason for being temporarily broke and needing a place to stay. But the cardinal rule is, never look too eager to accept money. Even if you're absolutely broke, you have to refuse the first offer of a loan, and say you never take money from a woman.

"One more question," I said.

"Give it up, Buttercup. We've talked enough about this."

"Just one last question! I promise!" I took a deep breath. "When someone took you home to their place after having bought your bullshit story, how did you ... you know?"

"No, I don't know." Your voice was almost prim.

"You know, do *it*. I mean, I'm sure the one you ended up with wasn't always let's say your physical type. I mean, as a man, how did you do it?"

Eyes flaring, voice cold, you answered: "Oh that's easy, Sandra. When someone buys your story, you feel *contempt*."

* * *

They approached her now, the woman first, Curly following close behind, holding a glass of water. Sandra gazed at her dead BlackBerry as if she were reading a funny message from her friend, then slipped it face down in her lap as Curly set the glass in front of her, spilling it slightly.

"Thank you," she said.

Hands crammed into her coat pockets, the woman indicated the café with an irritable shrug of her shoulder. "Here!"

"No, thank you. I'm good *here*," Sandra replied evenly. A sharp, familiar smell pierced her nostrils. Moonshine, Uncle Stanislaw's homemade brew, that reeking staple of family gatherings, pervasive while she was growing up. From the look of his florid face, she guessed it was emanating from Curly.

The woman shifted to her other foot, looking flummoxed as to what to do next, trying to size up this strange western woman who had not budged from her chair. Curiosity softened her hard, broad features, and Sandra saw that the woman wasn't as old as she had initially thought. Probably closer to her age, which she referred to as "fifty, and then it gets fuzzy," but she couldn't imagine this woman ever having long, shiny hair, or wearing even a smidgen of lipstick. It was if she had emerged from the womb like this, with her grey bun and clumpy shoes, the perfect party comrade.

Half needing to convince herself that she had not imagined the booking she had made this morning with Lucazs, she held up her brochure and pointed to the picture of what she hoped was her B&B.

"See? I'm staying here. Do you know where it is?"

The woman shrugged with a cultivated blank look. Curly, who had slunk behind her as if awaiting instructions, at least had the decency to look guilty, for Sandra had given him a generous tip after her harrowing cab ride down here. Did he spend it all on booze? What was his relationship with this steamrolling woman whose hands were still jammed into her pockets so that if there was a ring, it wasn't visible? Terminally cowed husband? Partner in clumsy heists perpetrated on anyone dumb enough to end up here?

The surrounding houses seemed to huddle together in a clannish way, their hollow black windows feeling like an accusation. Why did you have to come here and make trouble? Forcing us to look the other way, interrupting a day that had been turning out to be normal. You're an outsider, not from here, and aren't our problems always caused by people not from here? Bad enough dealing with the Nazis, the Communists, and the secret police—now we have spoiled western yuppies demanding we go the extra mile?

Another wave of panic hit. Maybe Lucazs was in on it as well. He had given her a beaming smile on the way out but, as she had learned, the smile of a handsome young man could have many meanings. Perhaps he was secretly sympathetic to the "people from the dark ages." Maybe he had been insulted by the unintentional condescension in her compliment about him "going the extra mile." A much-stomped-upon country, finally getting back on its feet after enduring some of the worst atrocities of the 20th century, being put upon to do more for people who were utterly clueless about their suffering. He must have seen her limping slightly when she signed out at the front desk. For all she knew, he could have planned the heist. *Stupid, old bitch arriving about two. And easy pickings! A lame duck!*

Looking queasy, Curly leaned closer to her, hesitated, and then lunged under the table for her luggage, throwing himself off balance. Sandra braced herself for him to vomit all over her in the wild stereotype of a drunken Pole, but the woman yanked him back with a sneering curse.

"Here!" she barked at Sandra again.

"No. I already have a B&B."

The woman then started cursing her with a fusillade of swear words that Sandra vaguely recognized from booze-soaked family Christmases while growing up, those shrill splutterings over some age-old family feud escalating to a fever pitch.

Just give up your BlackBerry, she thought, her mind racing. It's no big deal, it doesn't work. Maybe they'll see it as a haggle from the black market era, one sort of bargain exchanged for another.

Another oath split the air, and this time Sandra caught

something personal in the tone. Condescension. Yes, the woman had sensed something about her when she was sizing her up. The single woman, without a pack. No special man to come home to, and no hope anymore that there ever will be one. Tears sprang to Sandra's eyes, the last thing she needed this woman to see. Looking away, she pushed her luggage further under the table with her feet, which only succeeded in making the woman shove Curly back toward her. A mistake, for the sharp motion made him gag, and clamping his hand over his mouth, he stumbled back to the café.

It was then that Sandra saw the woman's hands, the knuckles swollen to the size of walnuts. Arthritis, a shared affliction. But rheumatoid arthritis, far more debilitating and painful, bathing small joints in an inflammatory broth until a hand became an immobile claw that was incapable of even grasping the handle of a suitcase.

"Fuck you," she said as the claws came toward her, intending to hit her, shove aside the table, she didn't know what. And raising her Blackberry high, she whacked it against the knuckles.

* * *

When my affliction rolled in, I was oddly grateful for the pain. At least that constant and often excruciating ache kept me from obsessing about what we eventually did *down there*. An edgy lover, you were pushing me past my boundaries, making me drunk with exhilaration at my new daring.

"Hey you. Is there something wrong?" I asked one night, when we were watching a movie at my place.

"No, nothing's wrong."

"You seem distracted."

"No ... ah, well yes, there is something, but I don't want to talk about it."

After much wheedling, I got it out of you. Your beloved 12-year-old daughter, whom I had met on a few occasions, needed braces, which you couldn't afford right now. The kids at school were starting to call her "Chiclet Mouth," and she was coming home crying, which was making you crazy.

"Oh, that's just terrible. How much are the braces?"

"$5,000. And that's just the start apparently. Now the dentist is telling us that her jaw is too small, and she may need reconstructive surgery."

"Can't your ex help?"

"Don't even go there. The bank is cancelling her credit cards."

The movie was a civil war romance from the '30s, and I watched as a carriage pulled up in front of a plantation.

"Would it help if I loaned you the money?"

You winced as if slighted. "I only told you about this because you asked what was bothering me, not because I was asking for a loan."

"I know. I know ..."

"It's a bad time for my cash flow right now, but I'll get the money."

"What if I loaned you half? That's $2,500."

"You can spare that much right now?"

"Yeah, I can. My business is doing well."

"I suppose that could get her started on a retainer, at least."

"Look, it's not a problem at all. I can even write a cheque for you right now."

I was halfway to my purse hanging in the adjoining hallway when you shouted: "No!"

"No 'what'?"

You had readjusted your position, perching on the couch's edge, rubbing the tops of your thighs in quick, frantic motions.

"No, I don't want your money. I don't take money from women."

I froze.

"Isn't that one of the lines from your con man repertoire?"

"What?"

"You know. Remember you told me the first rule of thumb was to say you never accepted money from a woman?"

Your face changed to that of a chastened child.

"Oh shit!" you cried. But at least you spared me the further insult of a canned apology as I showed you the door.

* * *

And now people were emerging from the arched alleyway into the square. Coming home from work, probably from a factory outside town as she had suspected. A man in a crumpled cap. A tank-like woman with a jutting prow of a bust clutching a loaf of French bread under her arm. No one looking her way, as Curly and the woman approached her, a new aggressiveness in their stride.

She couldn't believe that she'd hit the woman, had caused her to double over in startled pain. Seeing his partner lurching back to the café, whimpering and rubbing her hand had probably instantly sobered Curly up. Giving up the BlackBerry was out of the question.

You've got to make a move, she thought. But where? Who? Which of the inhabitants of this much-brutalized place who were now assiduously ignoring her, and justifiably so, wanting to get back to their hard-won, normal dinners, would help her?

She chose the woman with the prow-like bust, if only because she reminded her of her grandmother. Grasping the edge of the table to steady herself, it struck her, with a bizarre, disembodied irony, that she had achieved her wish to see the real Poland. On the run from some invader, a bullet meant for the head blasting the kneecap to a bloody pulp instead. Having to make that split-second decision of where to go for help. Perhaps your last thought ever as you made a mad dash across a cobblestone square, the ultimate leap of faith.

Her leg quivered, then buckled under her, much to the vindicated amusement of the woman, who let out a short barking laugh as Sandra fell back into her chair. A piercing, electronic shriek filled the air.

"Sandra?"

"Lucazs?"

"Yes, it is Lucazs, Sandra. I've been trying to phone you."

"My BlackBerry wasn't working! It's just come back on now!"

"Where are you, Sandra?"

"I don't know where I am, Lucazs! I have no idea where I am!"

"The lady from the B&B has been phoning me. She's been saying I am seeing this lady, I think she is the right lady, sitting at the table, but I don't know why she won't come."

Sandra saw a woman waving at her from a lace-curtained window. "Yes! Yes! I see her! Hello! It's me!"

People in the crowd began to stop, shy, curious looks on their faces. The woman spat on the cobblestones and turned away. Curly didn't follow. He extended his arm toward Sandra with the slightest of bows, as if reclaiming some kind of chivalry, long-lost in his Polish man's soul. "Come. I will help you," he said.

Dirty Laundry

*P*eter's shirts hung on the clothesline, arms dangling limply down as if begging forgiveness from a higher power. One faded denim, two flannel plaids, and a dark blue dress shirt, all stretched tautly on the bottom, swaying in the breeze.

I stood watching them from the window of the empty ground floor apartment in our house, which Kathleen, a young law student, had rented until a few weeks ago. Her abrupt, angry departure still echoed around me, all traces of habitation excised save for a few lone dust balls. Unlike our previous tenants, Kathleen had never invited us in, so what I knew about her furnishings came from those rare occasions when her blinds were open, allowing me to pick out the odd, scant detail: a vase of roses on the mantelpiece, a Picasso poster, textbooks stacked on Ikea shelves.

A gust of wind caught under the dress shirt, the one Peter likely would wear if he had to go to court. Usually it was dry-cleaned, but now that we faced the possibility of an unimaginably large fine ...

I flinched as a car pulled into the driveway—Peter,

home early from his design studio. When he got out of the car, I drew away from the window in case he came around back and saw me standing there—making me realize, for the first time, how exposed a single woman could feel living alone on the ground floor, and why Kathleen had immediately put up venetian blinds in the small study that overlooked the patio.

But no, Peter wasn't coming around the back. Instead, he unlocked the front door, checked the mail, then climbed the stairs in an anxious, half-halting way to the second-floor apartment where we lived. My stomach clenched in anger, followed by a dry heave of guilt born of my own possible collusion in this whole mess.

"Did he ever say anything inappropriate about Kathleen?" our lawyer had asked.

My gaze went to the patio, then back to Peter's shirts. This apartment would have to be rented as soon as possible to generate cash flow. I thought about this time the previous year, when Kathleen was deliberating whether to take this place, her arms clasped high across her chest, defensively gripping herself at the elbows.

"You'll feel safe here," I had said. "It's a pretty good neighbourhood. People look out for each other."

* * *

We bought our house, a three-story, red brick Victorian, when the market was high. At the time, having a rental property made sense, as we envisioned charging ever-escalating rents to our tenants to help pay off the mortgage. Instead, our tenants inevitably became friends, which made us reluctant to raise their rents. When our favourite and longest-staying tenants, a lesbian couple, moved to another city, we placed an ad in the newspaper: "One bedroom apartment in High Park. Fireplace. Study. Laundry facilities." Even with Toronto's ridiculously low vacancy rate, the flood of calls for our Saturday Open House took us by surprise. Forced to be decision makers, a role neither of us relished, Peter and I interviewed more than 20 prospective candidates, obliging them to fill out an application listing current employment and two references.

Kathleen was one of the last to arrive. Standoffish, a little shy, and frustrated, I suspected, after a day of scouring High Park only to find that the better places with Queen Anne façades and Georgian turrets were unaffordable. She was attractive in a reserved, preppie way, her white, tailored blouse and taupe pants making her look slightly older than the articling student she was. Somewhat giddy from a day of interviewing people, we had shown off the apartment, Peter emitting his raucous laughter with the natural flirtatiousness of a man used to having women respond to him. Kathleen didn't, I was glad to see, because who needed a tenant 20 years her junior coming onto her husband? Not that I was insecure about our marriage, but I often wondered if I did enough to keep Peter happy, to "keep the spark alive," as they constantly preached in women's magazines. With a deliberation that set her apart from the other candidates, Kathleen said she would like to think about the place a bit. Not interested, we thought; but then an hour later she returned with a cheque and said she would like to place a deposit. Looking back, I can see that her decisiveness had relieved us of the task of having to choose from other desirable candidates. And so, we said yes. In our haste to finalize the arrangemuits, we later realized we had forgotten to get a lease. "Oh well," Peter said, noting that one of Kathleen's references was a senior partner at a prestigious law firm. "If something goes wrong, I'm sure she'll find some way to sue us."

* * *

As I said, we had become good friends with our previous tenants, often getting together for coffee or barbecues. But with Kathleen, there was little conversation, not even a complaint about a leaky faucet. Nevertheless, we became unconsciously attuned to the sounds of her morning shower and the front door opening when she came home from work, late, around eleven. Most weekends she was away, visiting her boyfriend, a lawyer in Waterloo.

We shared the laundry facilities in the basement, which was only accessible from the patio. A clothesline ran from the top of Kathleen's back porch to the garage. In nice weather, I used it almost daily between breaks in my freelance writing, luxuriating in the smell of freshly dried laundry.

And so, one sunny weekday afternoon, clutching a hamper loaded with dirty laundry, I clomped out onto the patio—completely startling Kathleen, who was stretched out on a lawn chair, studying. She was wearing a pink, scooped-neck-T-shirt and fitted white shorts, which seemed all the more revealing because I had only previously ever seen her in dark pantsuits. Her legs were long, lithe, and very pale. A heavy black law book sat in her lap, open to a page in the middle. Struck by a feeling of having blundered into someone's privacy, I came to an abrupt stop.

Kathleen barely acknowledged me. Although I prided myself on being able to talk to anyone, I suddenly found myself tongue-tied. My eyes darted to the steps that led to the basement, down to my hamper, then back to her lap.

"What a beautiful day!" I finally chirped.

"Yes," was all she replied.

"One of the great things about being a freelancer," I said, suddenly feeling the need to impress upon her that I wasn't unemployed (for, during our few exchanges, she had never once asked me what I did for a living), "is being able to find time in your day to do your laundry."

The edges of her mouth pressed up in a thin smile.

"Are you studying?" I asked.

Kathleen closed her book over one thumb and, almost imperceptibly, drew her knees closer together. "I have an exam tomorrow."

"Ah! And it was so nice out that you decided to study out here!" I exclaimed, realizing, even as I was speaking, that it sounded too familiar. Overcome with a self-consciousness I hadn't felt in years, I gripped the hamper and stared foolishly at the contents. Socks. Shorts. A couple of Peter's and my faded denim shirts, the arms looped together in a sweetly affectionate way. The clothesline, running just above Kathleen's head, ignited by sunlight, was a thin neon tube. A perfect day for drying clothes outside, but Kathleen (who, despite my subtle hints about saving on energy bills, had yet to ever use the clothesline) could thwart that plan with her presence in the yard.

I modulated my voice to make it sound more proper. "I

trust everything is all right in your apartment? The appliances all working?"

Her chin tilted up in a stiff nod. I waited for her to make some polite reciprocal small talk to let me get on with my task but, whether out of shyness, social ineptness, or sheer annoyance at being intruded upon, she remained silent. Once again, I felt my eyes being drawn to her legs, the graceful way they tapered from her slim hips. I remembered Peter had once joked that nothing turned a man's crank like young flesh, and was glad that I was the one who had caught Kathleen dressed like this, and not him.

The silence became awkward, charged with what felt like hostility. Then I became aware that Kathleen was scanning the contents of my hamper, no doubt judging our comfortably faded clothes as slovenly and old-hippyish. Peter and I hadn't had children, and it occurred to me that this had stunted our perceptions, in that we tended to assume that young people viewed us peers rather than oldsters of their parent's age. Seeing ourselves as she saw us —Peter paunchy and graying, me with lines deepening around my once-admired doe eyes—was disconcerting. Trying not to sound officious, I resumed my landlady's voice.

"If there's ever a problem with one of the appliances, give us a call and Peter will come and fix it. He's pretty good with fridges."

"Everything's fine," Kathleen said, opening her book again.

"Well then! I'll get out of your way now! I'll just throw these into the washer and go back to writing my annual report!"

* * *

"She's so bloody uptight," I fumed to Peter later that night. I was still resentful that, out of respect for Kathleen's privacy, I had ended up using the dryer (even though after our encounter, she had sequestered herself in her study and drawn the blinds).

Peter was slouched in front of his computer, designing an ad layout. "Just the type you want to defile," he said, without turning around.

"What do you mean by that?" I was genuinely curious, for the warped vagaries of a man's sexuality fascinated me now that I wasn't killing myself trying to satisfy them.

"Oh, I don't know. Bring them down a peg or two."

"Oh, spare me your dirty mind!"

* * *

"Did he ever say anything inappropriate about Kathleen?" our lawyer had asked.

I had never been a particularly good liar. Under her probing gaze, my eyes shifted from her framed Osgood Hall degree to her long, manicured fingernails, which were painted a bright coral pink, a surprisingly coquettish touch for a middle-aged professional.

"I think ... well, I assume he found her attractive ... as most men find twenty-five-year-olds," I added defensively. "But to me, he said nothing I would find inappropriate."

"How would you describe your relationship?"

"Well, of course, after twelve years of marriage, it's not the same. But we haven't had affairs or anything."

She arched one eyebrow." Would you say your sexual relationship is ... satisfactory?"

I stared dumbly at her fingernails. Not according to the

proliferation of articles in women's magazines with titles like "Does your marriage need Viagra?", their earnest research suggesting that long-term marriages needed at least 2.5 amorous couplings a week, the onus being on the woman to initiate them.

"It is for me," I answered.

The truth was, I knew I had never satisfied Peter sexually. He had been a womanizer in his youth, his relationships tumultuous, charged with the eroticism of breaking up and making up, the woman ending up humiliated while he got away unscathed. When we met in our early thirties, he was caught in a cycle of dead-end scenarios, needing a woman to say, "Stop!" and really mean it.

I wasn't frigid. Nor did I consider myself a prude. But an element of raw lustiness, the truly profane, had always been lacking in me (although in the beginning of any relationship, I always did a good job of playing the part). Over the years, our sex life may have dwindled below the national average, but I was convinced that our relationship had evolved into a richer companionship—not quite the dreaded "brother and sister," but rather a deepening closeness that was hard to define. Besides, in my mid-forties, I was tired of the articles on how to please men. Peter's joke about nothing turning a man's crank like young flesh was true, I thought. I was tired of feigning an avidity that had never been there in the first place. The need to be relentlessly alluring at all times had passed, and for me, it was a relief.

Did he ever say anything inappropriate about Kathleen?

From time to time. And I didn't discourage it, for it seemed essential to keep us from becoming eunuchs, to maintain his bad-boy myth.

* * *

Landlords who respect their tenant's privacy can still be privy to personal information, such as what comes in the mail. All of it went into a basket in the front hall. When I collected ours, I always gave the tenants' a cursory scan, on the lookout for unpaid bills marked "urgent," overdue credit card notices, things that could jeopardize rent payment.

One day after work, Peter bounded up the stairs, beaming. "Did you see what Kathleen got in the mail today?"

I frowned. When I came across the *Victoria's Secret* catalogue in the mail earlier that afternoon, I had thought it was for me, that some company had put me on their mailing list. For a split second, it made me feel girlish, that someone should think I could wear all those racy bras and panties. Then I saw Kathleen's name on the address label, and a bad feeling had crept in. Hoping that Peter wouldn't see it, I set it at the bottom of the mail basket, then carefully covered it with a telephone bill, a Sears Scratch and Save coupon, and a flyer for a new Pizza Pizza special.

Peter chortled. "I always knew that Kathleen was into sexy lingerie!"

"Oh?"

"How come you don't wear underwear like that anymore?"

"I don't think I'd look quite the same as Kathleen in it," I said, although that wasn't quite the truth. Slackening off sexually didn't mean I had let myself go—I was still able to fit into a size small. I waited for Peter to refute what I had just said, but he was spellbound, grinning as if he had just won the lottery.

"Now, don't you be getting your mind in the gutter," I chided out of old habit.

His green eyes flashed, hinting at the attractiveness that had captivated me in the beginning, when I felt that I had caught myself a prize, tamed a wild beast.

"Oh, not me! Never!"

* * *

We had a loosely established laundry schedule: weekdays for me because of my work flexibility, and weekends for Kathleen. Late one Sunday afternoon, while I was chopping herbs for a marinade, Peter came out of the bedroom clutching a hamper that was spilling over with ripped jeans and old sweatshirts—virtually discarded clothes that he must have ferreted out from the deepest reaches of our closet.

"I think Kathleen is doing her laundry," I said. I had caught a glimpse of her from the kitchen window a few minutes earlier, scuttling down the basement steps with her hamper, which, of course, had a closed lid. "I can wash those things tomorrow."

Peter's voice rose in insistent, boyish protest. "But I have nothing to wear to work tomorrow!"

Do it later, I began to say, then stopped. "Well, go on then. But try not to get in her way."

The laundry room was cramped, with barely enough room to squeeze one person between the washer and dryer. And sometimes when I'm in my daze of vacillating emotions, both dodging and examining what I can only refer to as "the incident," I'll flash on what likely happened. After returning from a weekend with her boyfriend, Kathleen would have tossed all the clothes from her duffle bag into her hamper—hastily, without separating delicates from the machine washables.

She would have just started transferring them into the washer when Peter barged in on her with his hulking hamper, plunking it down next to hers, apologizing with his blustery laughter. I could picture Kathleen freezing, flattening herself against the washer as she considered the best way to manoeuvre past him. Somehow she excused herself and darted back into her apartment. Was it then that Peter spotted the sheer lace, pink panties peeking out from the hamper she had forgotten to close?

And then what? Had he scooped them out? Pressed them to his skin? Sniffed them? I don't know the details, nor do I care to. All I know is that he spied them and must have felt a surge of unbearable longing. Then, maybe thinking he heard Kathleen coming back, he panicked, and stuffed them into his pocket.

I found them the next morning in my underwear drawer, taken aback by the sight of pink lace next to my sensible black cotton. I knew instantly what had happened; felt shock, then shame, and then a sense of the inevitable— that with a man like Peter, I would eventually have to deal with some form of mid-life crisis, and here it was.

He was hunched in front of his computer, intently fiddling with a layout before heading off to work.

"Did you take these?"

His shoulders jerked up. "They're not yours?"

Oh the pang of having to accept that lie, both of us knowing that I hadn't worn anything remotely like these panties in years.

"They belong to Kathleen."

His guilt-stricken nod was quickly replaced by what has become his mainstay with our lawyer—vehement denial. "I thought they were yours, honey! I didn't think you would want them in the wash!"

They had an embroidered heart design in the sheer lace of the crotch, and a thong of shiny satin. My heart became pinched high up in my chest, where it has been ever since.

"We'll have to put them back," I said.

Peter nodded, then turned to his layout. We had reverted to our roles; him the bad boy, me, the censor who didn't give into base urges, and who now had to tidy up after his negligence.

In retrospect, I should have just disposed of them, let Kathleen think that she had misplaced them somewhere. But they were too beautiful to throw away, no doubt ordered, after much loving deliberation, from *Victoria's Secret*. I spent the better part of the day agonizing over what to do.

Knocking on her door and returning them, as I would have with our previous lesbian tenants (their brightly coloured underpants, announcing their sexual orientation through the rainbow colors of the gay coalition, had sometimes shown up in our wash), was out of the question, as was phoning a friend for advice. Eventually I decided to make it look as if they had fallen out of her hamper while she was loading things into the washer.

Rarely had Kathleen come home early. At four o'clock, I scooted down to the laundry room, her panties balled up in my hands. Crouching in front of the washer, I made a few frantic—and ultimately time-wasting—attempts at authenticity, trying to insert them between the washer and dryer, with just a bit peeking through.

I've noticed that some willowy women have a light, almost soundless step. Kathleen was no exception. First I saw her navy pumps stationed in the doorway, then the sharp centre pleat of her trousers. Not fully registering what was happening, I grabbed the panties and stood up slowly, steadying myself on the washer and dryer.

"Oh, hello! We found these in the laundry! I guess they belong to you!"

There was a long, incriminating silence, during which Kathleen squared her shoulders and blinked at me through narrowed eyes. Finally her voice came out, clipped and authoritative, making me remember that she was, in fact, a law student.

"How did they get there?"

"I guess Peter must have taken them by mistake." *Peter?* I actually said his name? "This used to happen with our other tenants," I said, setting the panties on the side of the washer. "The gay ones! Their underwear would get into our hamper!"

Kathleen wadded the panties into one hand and withdrew it behind her back. "This is theft."

"Theft? No, we didn't take anything! Like I told you, this used to happen with our other tenants ..."

Another pause, a hissing intake of breath. "With *your* husband, I'm sure it did."

* * *

I assumed that Kathleen would move out, if not immediately, then at least within the month, and was fully prepared to offer her the last month's rent. The possibility that she would launch a sexual harassment suit against Peter never entered my head. But, as our lawyer explained, this type of claim hinged upon one party being in a position of power and, as a landlord, Peter had a key to her apartment. In effect, Kathleen was accusing him of using his key to let himself into her apartment and rifle through her drawers. For this, she was suing us for a year's back rent, moving costs, expenses for her own lawyer, and emotional damages. The grand tally, which on top of our lawyer's fees, made my mind reel.

This, according to our lawyer, was the worst-case scenario, and most likely we would have to come up with a year's back rent. Peter's assertion that it was an unforgiveable but honest mistake was plausible, given that I could have probably fit into the panties. And, with a lot of effort on my part, we might even be perceived as a couple that upheld the national average of having sex 2.5 times a week.

***

Peter's shirts bellied up on the clothesline. Above me, I could hear him pacing from room to room in our apartment, fretting, perhaps wondering if I was going to leave him. Would I? Did I want to stay with a guy who got his kicks from panties? (But only panties for god's sakes, not child porn!) Was it worth giving up this house, this lifestyle, and a twelve-year emotional investment to start over again as a single woman in her forties? (*But did he sniff them, did he actually sniff?*)

His shirt sleeves kicked up in unison, as if choreographed to put on a cheerful dance. They were completely dry now, with that fresh outdoor smell in which I used to take such stupid joy. Peter's pacing became louder, and I didn't want to think how menacing that could sound. Stepping out onto the porch, I reached for the clothesline, and began pulling the bobbing shirts toward me.

Valentine

$\sim\!\!\infty\!\!\sim$

*H*olly opened an art file called "Broken Hearts" and watched as they appeared on her computer screen. Slackened pulmonary arteries. Swollen ventricular chambers. Bruised aortas. A collection of cardiac parts in various states of disease and distress, all rendered with the improbable calm of a classical painting. She was a medical illustrator with clients all around the world. Her latest assignment, for a Swiss pharmaceutical company, was to show how a new drug could dissolve arterial plaque. Clicking onto a half-finished drawing of an artery, she enlarged it so that it looked like a corridor. Then she began the meticulous task of lining its walls with plaque, making them look like gritty plaster deposits that could never be scraped off.

Her studio was on the third floor of her house, insulated in a dense winter quiet that permeated the soft jazz playing in the background. As she drew platelet after platelet, the silence pressed in. Then she heard the front door open; her daughter Nicole home from school.

"Nicky. Up here," she called, printing out what she had done so far on her new printer. It sat on a shelf next to plastic models of the skull, heart, and intestines. To lessen their macabre effect ("It's like the set of a slasher film in here," her ex-husband Carl had once remarked), she had added deliberately arty touches. Plants. Posters. Homemade pots in upbeat colours that couldn't remotely suggest blood.

"How was school?" she asked, when Nicole appeared, conscious that her voice had the eager bounce of someone who hadn't spoken to anyone for hours.

Nicole shrugged. She was fourteen. Submerged, as usual, in a pair of mammoth overalls that puddled into lumpen folds at her feet, stunting her height by several inches. Slouched in the door frame, she reminded Holly of an overgrown toddler waiting to be set in a Jolly Jumper.

"A good day? Bad?" Holly prompted.

"It was all right," Nicole replied vaguely. "Are you working on the computer tonight?"

"I don't have to. Why?"

"I need to use your new printer."

"Not a problem." Nicole had her own computer, which contained, Holly suspected, but never asked, secret journals divulging her feelings about the divorce three years ago.

"What are you printing?"

"A card," Nicole said, then hesitated. "A Valentine's card."

"God. Is that here already?" Holly asked, although she was well aware of the assault of cupids and hearts in store windows.

"Two weeks."

Holly restrained herself from asking whether the card was for anyone special. So far Nicole and her friends had shown no signs of being interested in boys—not that Holly was certain what these signs would be. (Or maybe she didn't really want to know, the topic being too close to her own predicament of thinking of starting to date again at an age well past her "best before" date.) But she imagined that interest would involve wardrobes more beguiling than their group uniform of asexual overalls.

What did her daughter's body look like under all that cloth, she wondered. Nicole had become very private of late, undressing only behind closed doors. The cropped tops she occasionally wore revealed no jutting ribs, ruling out at least, the likelihood of an eating disorder.

"Do you want some help with the printing? The printer still has a few bugs."

"No, I can do it," Nicole murmured, heading downstairs, leaving Holly with her magnified artery. Almost finished, it looked like a calcified catacomb, access narrowed to a slit. Just like my own feelings, she thought grimly, adjusting the hue. And there was no wonder drug that could open them up.

* * *

Holly could become lost in these drawings, awed at the infinite diversity of an anatomical structure: a cell, which up close became a landscape with shapes resembling rivers, lakes and forests. She was glad of this, for she felt self-conscious about her work, even embarrassed at the science geek associations. But drawing was something she did well. Even as a child she could replicate life around her, a skill she didn't show off, but pragmatically honed, like typing to be used at a later date. She'd been in arts at university when she met Carl, a shy, civic-minded graduate student with an unfinished thesis on racial biases. When he went into law, she switched to medical illustration, a lucrative specialty that could support them until he finished his degree. It also enabled her to be a stay-at-home mom. It doesn't get any better than this, she often thought in the halcyon early days of their marriage, Nicole in her playpen behind the art table, teething on a piece of plastic intestine. When Carl would come home, frazzled by the transition from academe to the corporate world, he would hug her and gratefully murmur: "My rock."

But rocks can be moved whether they like it or not. She had sensed something was wrong one December. It was a foreboding that activated a frantic cheeriness, made her bake too many Christmas cookies, put up too many outdoor lights blinking out their bright message of alarm.

"We've become like brother and sister," he had told her.

Holly had been making marzipan, rolling tiny balls of dough into coconut. All she could think of was the underpants she was wearing—beige, well-worn—and how she wished she were wearing one of her lacy pairs (although she wasn't sure they fit anymore, confirming his opinion that she had let herself become too comfortable).

"Is there someone else?" she had asked.

"A woman I work with. Another lawyer. You don't know her."

"Let me guess. One of those young, fast-track women who works and plays just as hard as the boys."

Carl had been fingering coconut flakes between his thumb and forefinger, one by one, like a rosary. There was a long silence, then his voice caught with a dark protectiveness.

"No, she's not that type of woman at all. She reads poetry. She can quote Rilke."

Holly had made the divorce clean and easy. She had seen

a look in his eyes that went beyond pain, guilt, or sorrow. It was pity. He felt pity that someone with her solid sensibilities would never know the love that had the power to break up a secure marriage. She had wanted to get out of range of his dramatic love, which by its very nature would devalue the one that had come before it. More importantly, she didn't want Nicole exposed to it. Not when she was about to become a teenager, a precarious time for self-worth—especially if you were female.

* * *

The next day Holly found herself experiencing another type of discord; her heart file wouldn't open. And the client had phoned asking to see the artery illustrations. She pulled down various files looking for the problem. Then a window came up saying it was with the printing port. Of course—Nicole printing out her Valentine's card last night had probably screwed something up. After a hopeful bout of clicking, the printing icon returned to normal. But when Holly opened her file, another image rushed up at her.

At first she thought it was soft porn from an Internet site. Some weird transmigration that must have occurred while she was tinkering with it. There were two photos of a woman in bed wearing a black bra, garter, panties, stockings, and heels. Her face was covered by a heart. In the one photo, she was lying on her stomach, hands under her chin, legs crossed coyly at the ankles; in the other, she was seated with her breasts thrust out in an exaggerated cheesecake pose. Beneath the photos was a caption. It read: "How would you like me this Valentine's Day? Over easy? Or sunny side up?"

She realized it was Nicole when she recognized the

bedpost. The one they had found at a garage sale and sponge-painted together. Barely breathing, she took in the figure that had lately been hidden from her. Taut waist. Small breasts. Long thighs that swelled tulip-like at the top giving every indication that they would one-day bulge like Holly's. And a pert little detail—the garter belt had bows at the side. Slowly enlarging the head, she saw that the heart had been cut out of red cardboard, and pasted over the face after the photo was taken, in a hurry evidently, because glue showed at the sides. Her heart began to race, sharp palpitations that nicked her chest wall. Then she shut down the computer, and let herself be swallowed up in its harsh after-hum.

* * *

After Carl married the lawyer he left her for, he moved to Ottawa to take a prestigious government job. Nicole visited him a few times a year, and afterwards, Holly would resist the urge to probe for too many details about his new life. Too much potential for classless behaviour: obsessing, devising put-downs, (although she was pleased that an English professor friend considered Rilke a "sentimental" poet), and most demeaning, being goaded into desperate one-upmanship by latching herself onto any (if any) available male. As far as relationships went, she considered herself closed for repairs. Something of the good role model in this, she thought. Rebuilding, not blaming, taking time to heal, and emerging, she hoped, with some wisdom for the pain.

"We have to talk," she now said to Nicole who was slumped in an armchair in the family room watching TV.

Nicole nodded, stiffening at the over-rehearsed quality

in Holly's voice. Once again she was submerged in cloth: flood pants and an oversized lumberjack shirt, the collar of which brushed her tips of her ears. With her hair pulled back, her face was moon round, the burgeoning cheekbones still layered in baby fat. *How would you like me this Valentine's Day? Over easy? Or sunny side up?*

"I found your card in my computer. Apparently, when you used the printer it screwed up something on the hard drive and got into my files."

Nicole sank deeper into the chair, and crossed her arms tightly around her chest.

"I don't know what to ask first. Who was it for? Are you having a relationship with this person? Is this what four-teen-year-old girls do these days, send cards like this?"

"It was a joke," Nicole blurted, shamed and hostile.

"A joke."

"I was just fooling around. I didn't send it."

But you posed for it, Holly thought. When I was out, or even when I was upstairs in my studio. Snapping on garters while I was hunkered over an arid artery drawing. The thought of having to deal with this, when she had already dealt with so much, gave rise to a new rage. Focusing on a plaid pocket that puffed up from Nicole's crossed arms, she asked: "Where did you get the lingerie?"

"Not from your underwear drawer."

Holly flinched, then recovered. "Obviously not. You went out and bought it?" Nicole stared harder at the TV, an inane commercial with dancing cats. Holly wanted to march over and switch it off, except her legs had turned to plaster. Who was this guy (or boy—surely he wouldn't be more than sixteen?) who had gotten her daughter to wear garters and heels? He would no doubt be arrogant, blasé from the daily spectacle of girls throwing themselves at him, flaunting their neediness (and this is what upset her most; how could her daughter be so *obvious*?). Since the divorce, they had fallen into a polite reserve around each other—a shared pride, Holly thought, in not exposing one's wounds. Now an unsettling realization crept in. Maybe Nicole hadn't appreciated the stoic way she had left the marriage. Maybe she felt contempt that Holly hadn't fought for her man.

"We're going to have to talk about this again when we can both deal with it better," Holly said, her voice starting to shake.

"I told you I didn't send it. Just forget about it, OK?"

* * *

She had read somewhere that it took three years to heal after a divorce. Which seemed about right for her. It was not to be underestimated, a lengthy recovery period. There was absolution there, respecting the frailty of the hobbled ego, honouring lowered expectations, admitting you weren't up to certain things.

But her metaphorical retreat under the covers was ending. And the whole reason for taking time to heal seemed lost, like a computer file floating off into cyberspace. What she had emerged to was the probability that her adolescent daughter was having sex. And not just sex. Wild sex. Kinky sex. The kind that had always been slightly beyond Holly, and which mocked her hopes that Nicole's first boyfriend would be a nice, safe sort, non-threatening to both of them. Since their last exchange, they hadn't spoken to one another. But who could Holly talk to about this? Not Carl, who would judge her child-raising capabilities. Not her friends and family, with whom she was trying to appear more intact. And not herself, certainly not herself, because even thinking about the subject made her thoughts contract into an immobilized crouch.

"We've become like brother and sister," he had told her.

But the truth was, hadn't they always been? The question would bob up in her mind over the past three years, and she would push it back, refusing to let it surface. Now she wondered; had she been a kind of test run for Carl? Had she represented the shallow, safe end of the pool where he could practice growing into what he wanted to be, always knowing he could touch bottom until he had the confidence to venture out into deeper waters?

* * *

The silence between her and Nicole continued into the week. Then one afternoon after school, Holly heard her walking up to her studio, the slow, shambling step she used to rejoice in when the house was booming in emptiness. But it wasn't the same daughter anymore. It was one who was scaling the peaks of sexual cunning, who had judged her mother as not up to the challenge of keeping a man. Hardly a role model to aspire to. Holly was finishing the "after" part of her artery illustration, showing how the client's drug could dissolve plaque as easily as soap bubbles. When Nicole entered the room, she didn't turn, but focused more intently on the screen. Out of the corner of her eye she could see Nicole dawdling about with things on the shelves, picking up the plastic intestine model, setting it down.

"Do you have a moment?" Nicole finally asked.

"A moment. I have to get this drawing done."

"I want to talk about the Valentine's Day card."

Her voice collapsed on the last word, confused and lost. Holly faced her daughter, the effort of feigning composure pinching her mouth into a prim line. But was there anything to feel threatened about? Nicole slumped forlornly against the shelves, her hands crammed into the pockets of a pair of overalls, the crotch of which barely floated above the floor. The baggy shirt she wore with them made her body look not only shrunken, but flaccid too, as if all her bones had been removed. Nonetheless, Holly looked back at her computer, terrified of spotting a black bra strap peeking out from behind the shirt collar.

"All right. Talk," she said coldly.

"It was a joke."

"So you said."

"No. It wasn't what it seemed. I didn't even do it for guys. I did it for girls."

Are you going to tell me you're a lesbian? Holly panicked. Did this explain the tight-knit group, the wilfully asexual wardrobes?

"Oh no. It's not like that," Nicole blurted, seeing her look. "It was like this ... this ... dare we decided to do for Valentine's Day. Like a contest to see who could come up with the raunchiest card. We were going to send it to some guys we liked with our faces covered so they'd never know who it was. We were just fooling around."

"A dare? You did it on a dare?"

"Yeah. We didn't even send them out because ..." Her shoulders jerked as if suddenly poked. "Everything's gotten really weird between us."

It all poured out. A misunderstanding in the group. So-and-so not speaking to so-and-so; a typical teen tiff that could have been lifted from a '50s sitcom. The blurt-y incoherence of Nicole's speech, her raw distress about the disharmony between her friends brought Holly's guard down a little. Was there a chance she was telling the truth? Could it be peer pressure, rather than kinky sexual exploration that had led to this card? Nicole had always been a follower, deeply loyal to her friends, probably too eager to please. There was nothing in her carriage to suggest that she was anything other than what she appeared to be: an adolescent, temporarily unmoored from her peers, with no recourse but to reach out to her mother.

"So what you're saying is, you didn't send these cards?"

"No. I don't even know if we were going to. They were pretty embarrassing."

"Who took the picture of you?"

"I did. I put my camera on a tripod. I had to jump on and off the bed to set and reset it every time I did a pose. My face looked really stunned in the pictures. I'm glad it had a heart covering it."

"Did the other girls pose like you?"

Nicole flushed, and glanced away. "No. We all did different things." Holly nodded, shutting off images of crotch shots and leather collars. No, it was too much to absorb for now, the topic had to be closed, fast, fast.

"Was there any particular ... person you were going to send this card to?"

Another flush, this time deeper. "No ... not really."

"Where did you get the underwear?"

This last question (which Holly had not intended to

ask) hung in the air with a portentous weight as if it were the definitive answer to something. To her relief, Nicole screwed up her nose like a grossed-out child.

"From The Bay. I told the salesperson it was a gift so I got to take everything back but the panties. And that kind of made me mad because they cost like six bucks and I'm never going to wear them again. They felt ... so weird against my skin."

Of course it could all be a lie, Holly thought later as she clicked in the finishing touches on her drawing. A ruse devised by her sexually precocious daughter to lull her into a false sense of security, keep her off her back. It was past midnight, her studio throbbing with a disjointed quiet that comes from thoughts that won't stop spinning. Holly decided to accept for now that Nicole was telling the truth, that it was all misguided peer pressure. Not entirely innocent, but at least not malignant. The cyst that scares, but doesn't spread. A false alarm that might be hiding a deeper devastation—but for now, a reprieve.

She looked at her drawing, which depicted the inner lining of the artery after the drug's treatment. Plaque-free, clean as a whistle, the hard chrome of a car that had never been scratched. A fallacy, this. In real life, the artery would be pitted and pocked from scar tissue, its corroded surface always susceptible to more damage. Yet wasn't that the great lie about healing, she thought as she printed out the page. Sometimes it didn't mean getting well at all. Sometimes it just meant adjusting to another kind of pain.

Thick

Standing at the Kinko's counter, Jane Wilding found herself in the unprecedented position of waiting to be served. She had just driven two hours from her home in Collingwood for a modelling audition in the late afternoon and needed to get old photographs of herself colour-copied. Kinko's was an ice-blue cube in Toronto's Annex, half-filled with students milling around the self-serve machines. Leather portfolio in hand, she had headed toward the back counter where five young men were operating copiers. They absently glanced up as she approached, then looked back down at what they were doing. At the counter, she positioned herself under a sign saying "Orders" and waited for one, two, or three of the men to spring up and help her. But they calmly continued working, punching instructions on computer screens, unwrapping bricks of white paper, not paying attention. Newness in anything, whether country or culture, had always intrigued Jane. And with the detached curiosity of a tourist who has just entered unfamiliar terrain, she observed the novel panorama of a group of males who, to all intents and purposes, appeared to be oblivious to her.

Of course, she didn't expect to make the same impact she once had. The last article written about her four years ago for the Grey county paper said she looked the same but had "thickened." Such an ordinary word compared to the superlatives that had once been applied to her. Goddess. Fantasy woman. And in a flurry of mixed metaphors, a tribute to her lips in which the cleft above her upper lip was described as "the fulcrum in a swelling chorus of praise." Now, thickened? "At least they didn't say I was thick," she had laughed to her husband Derek, always sensitive about being perceived as another vapid model. As in previous interviews, she had tried to minimize talk about the way she looked, focusing instead on promoting her sister's country inn near Collingwood where she and Derek were working after a decade living abroad.

She set her portfolio on the counter. The clerk closest to her, a sandy-haired young man, glanced at a spot over her shoulder, then extracted a binder from a nearby shelf.

The place is busy, she told herself. Still, no place had ever been too busy for her before. In the past, with embarrassing regularity, spaces had always appeared in crowded hotels and restaurants, along with the occasional complimentary bottle of wine. She was dressed in her usual understated style; safari pants and shirt, granny glasses, hair pulled back. Now she found herself taking off her glasses and pushing them back on her head. No one rushed to serve her. The notion of having to draw attention to herself when she had spent her entire adult and adolescent life trying to fend it off, made her want to burst out laughing. What did one do? Clear one's throat? Say excuse me? The copiers continued their steady thrum, which seemed to exclude her. Slowly, and with surprised disbelief, Jane unzipped her portfolio and opened it so that a magazine cover showing her in a leopard-print bikini was clearly visible on the counter. The sandy-haired clerk was instantly before her.

"Can I help you?" he asked.

"I'll need a colour copy of this," she said, slipping the cover from the plastic portfolio pages. "Body shots," her agent, whom she hadn't heard from in years, had said when she called for this audition. "The more recent the better."

Reddish-pink patches appeared behind the clerk's ears. "Is that you?"

Jane shrugged. "The airbrushed, retouched version."

His hand hovered above the photo; he was momentarily too flustered to touch it. Now Jane was aware of the familiar stir, the other young men not concentrating on their work anymore, but stealing furtive glances at the work counter where she was setting out another bathing suit shot of herself.

"Do you still model?"

"Not if I can help it," she said with a grimace, trying not to think of how much she needed the job. Feeling ashamed about this (plus the easy way she had just drawn attention to herself), she turned, almost sternly, to an article about her conservation efforts in Nepal entitled "Beauty with a Cause."

"It looks like you got to see the world," the clerk said, smiling and picking up her bathing suit photos from the counter.

"Well, I didn't model for the intellectual stimulation," she said.

* * *

The question every interviewer used to ask was: "Had she been beautiful as a child?" Her reply was an adamant no. Her much-lauded full lips were not fashionable when she was growing up in the early sixties; in fact, they were regarded as a vulgarity in proper WASP society. She had inherited her lips from her grandmother, who had been a missionary in China, and whose legacy of adventurous good works Jane hoped to continue.

Although Nanna eschewed fashion, she took great pains to be decorous in public. "You might need this one day," she had said ruefully to Jane, passing her a yellowed clipping from a woman's magazine on "how to give generous lips the illusion of being less full."

The instructions were to blend liquid foundation not just over your face, but your lips too, draw in a smaller-sized mouth with a lip pencil, then carefully colour it in. Jane would never forget the look of Nanna's minimized mouth at social functions, the millimetres of unacceptable fullness crinkling under their cake-y camouflage. And she had wondered if this would be her fate as a woman, having to endure the obvious but necessary covering up of aberrant facial features.

Instead, adoration came straight at her with no warning. She was twelve years old, walking with her older sister along the beach on Lake Simcoe. Wearing a hand-me-down bathing suit she was outgrowing, but wasn't self-conscious about, because aside from her freak lips, she rarely thought of herself as anything other than one of the gangly, freckled Wilding girls. Up ahead of them stood a bunch of college guys. Something on the beach had caught their attention, something momentous. They all stood pillar-still, gazes riveted to the same spot.

At first, Jane couldn't make out their features. But drawing closer, she saw a pair of narrowed eyes go molten, a lower lip drop. Her. They were looking at her. Suddenly she knew where the bathing suit didn't fit: the tautness across her chest, the sides riding up her ever-lengthening legs. When she was a couple of feet away from the group, the best-looking guy grinned at her in a way that made her throat clutch, as he dropped to one knee. "Ooh. He loves you yeah, yeah, yeah!" he crooned right at her. She froze, her sister broke into a titter of high, confused laughter, and they ran off.

The camera loved her too, as one article gushed. Her first magazine cover, at 17, found her on a beach in Bali in a bathing suit that did fit, her much-fussed-over lips blooming like a hothouse flower on the page.

Just one year, she told herself. Make enough money to pay for a university degree, maybe in anthropology. One year became two, then three. By the time she was old enough to have graduated, she was being ridiculously well-paid for doing nothing more than tilting her hips and maintaining what she hoped would be interpreted as a self-mocking pout.

"Do you consider yourself a feminist?" was the second question every interviewer asked. Very much so, Jane would answer. How did one reconcile that with modelling bikinis? By not allowing oneself to be objectified. By refusing Hugh Hefner, who had asked her not once, but twice, to pose for *Playboy*. By dressing down in her personal life. By spurning the marriage proposals of nice, rich men who offered to take care of her, choosing instead moody men with a social conscience, who blew hot and cold sexually (thereby confirming her hope that she was loved for more than her looks). By being forever cognizant that her beauty had given her a free ride and that one day it would be over.

Her brand of feminism involved distancing herself from her image plastered all over the media. Disappearing into remote corners of the globe to purge herself of the adoration that came just from being. When an assignment took her to Nepal, she stayed on, becoming hostess at a jungle lodge—and officially ending, she thought, her modelling career. There she met Derek, a former stockbroker who had renounced materialism for Third World conservation. For ten years they lived the effortless altruism she had always believed to be her birthright, her wages helping to fund Derek's various social aid programmes. But when a reforestation programme went bust through mismanagement, they returned to Canada, broke, and settled at her sister's inn.

They had been working there for—could it be?—seven years? While Jane didn't mind the work (booking reservations, managing the bar, placating disgruntled guests), she found it disconcerting to still be there. "A hostess with the mostest," she grinned when people asked her what she did for a living. But it didn't have the same self-deprecating ring now that she was in her mid-forties.

Of greater concern was Derek. Since moving back to Canada, he had made a few attempts at forest preservation. But after reading an article about how the Amazon would be wiped out in 80 years if deforestation continued at its present rate, he pretty much gave up on everything. There is a Buddhist word for pilgrimage, gnasko, which means "going around to places in no haste and without particular destination," that she had once adopted as her personal creed. But lately she had the nagging sense that she had bumped up against a dead end: she was almost parasitically dependent on her sister.

The clerk returned with the colour copies of her younger self. He looked at her with desire and she didn't discourage it, surprised and dismayed by how much it boosted her confidence.

"What are you auditioning for?" he asked as she briskly slipped the copies back into her portfolio and zipped it up.

"Oh, nothing interesting." A "body shaper" her agent had said. A euphemism for a long-line girdle that would flatten the tush and tummy of a spreading middle-aged woman. A five thousand dollar fee that would ease her indebtedness to her sister and perhaps (although couldn't admit this to herself) lead to a few more jobs in the aging boomer category.

"I hope you get the work," he smiled, flushing brighter.

"If you call it work," she shrugged, momentarily strengthened by the reconnection to her old self, who could always take it or leave it.

* * *

The audition was on King Street in a converted warehouse. The photographer a Steve-somebody she'd never met. As she pulled into the parking lot, she felt the familiar distancing emotions of distaste and ambivalence. She took her portfolio from the front seat. It had felt odd putting it together, photos she hadn't seen in years and which, if it hadn't been for her sister diligently saving every magazine she appeared in, she wouldn't have kept at all. At least she could catch up with some of the models she used to work with, she rationalized as she headed into the building.

But when she stepped into the reception area, she thought she was in the wrong place. The dozen or so faces glancing up at her were young.

She approached a girl wearing an embroidered vest and patched jeans, an exaggerated hippie retro look that mocked sixties naiveté.

"Is this the audition for the Shaper's undergarment?" she asked.

A pair of vacant, unlined eyes blinked up at her. "Uh huh."

"I thought they were casting for older women."

"Oh, they are. I'm 26."

Jane wanted to laugh, imagining concocting this into a funny story when she got home. Instead, she felt her chest tighten, an unexpected buffeting of fear. She lowered herself into an empty chair beside the girl and frowned at the door to the photographer's studio, which was firmly shut.

"Do you know how long they're taking in there?"

"I don't know. I just got here."

Jane waited, then waited some more. It was a different kind of wait from the one at Kinko's, this one deliberate; an arrogant photographer taking his time, keeping all these good-looking women in his sway. Something that, in her goddess-status heyday, she had never put up with. Her anxiety rose, making her feel light-headed, and reminding her of those rickety Nepalese jungle planes she and Derek used to ride in, scouring the Himalayas for deforestation, bare patches attesting to the futility of their efforts. Another young woman waltzed in, her full lips unabashedly and poorly enhanced, like punched-in pillows. Her grand-mother's yellowed newspaper clipping floated to mind. How incredulous she would be that the lips so maligned in her generation would be so sought after in Jane's.

Thinking of her grandmother momentarily steadied Jane. Her greatest disappointment was that Nanna had died before she could see her fledging conservation efforts. "Beauty is as beauty does" was the only comment she'd make on the modelling. But didn't beauty do right? Or at least try to? And shouldn't there be some reward in that? Something that should have saved her from ever having to endure an audition like this?

"Jane Wilding?"

Jane started. A man with a fashionably shaved head and smooth poker face was introducing himself as Steve the photographer and motioning her into his studio. It was disorientingly bright, bleached lights bouncing off white backdrops, a web of black wires criss-crossing the floor. Without making small talk, he motioned for her to sit down across from him at a long desk along one wall. Jane un-zipped her portfolio and handed him the colour copies of herself, which he glanced at, then set down.

"Anything more recent?"

Jane shook her head, again taken aback by the lack of effect she was having on a male. Not that she expected a younger generation of photographers to know who she was, but still—she had never anticipated this indifference tinged with what felt like ... derision.

"I look the same but have thickened," she joked, trying to break the ice. He didn't smile. "My agent said you were looking for an older woman's body. More real."

His right eyebrow cocked up in a condescending arc.

"Indeed we are." He flipped open her portfolio and paused with mild interest at a face shot. "Great lips. Real?"

"Yes. I inherited them from my grandmother who was a missionary ..."

"Did she do it in the missionary position? Yuk. Yuk. Just kidding." Slapping her portfolio shut, he stood up and frowned at the lights. "OK. We're going to have to get a shot of your behind."

"My behind?"

He winced in a close approximation of embarrassment. "The clients aren't sure what they're looking for. They say they'll know it when they see it."

"My agent didn't tell me this," Jane said, her throat constricting.

"But she did tell you to bring some recent body shots, didn't she? These photographs are like ... 20 years old, right?"

Jane couldn't speak. For a second, she saw his eyes soften in pity, as if she were a slightly dotty relative he feared one day becoming. Then his voice became cold.

"Look, this is something I'm asking of most of the ladies today. No need to get your knickers in a knot. You get to keep them on."

* * *

Jane pulled toward an unmarked side road, wondering if it were the same one that led to Collingwood. Or should she have turned by that thin grove of trees she passed ten minutes before? She had taken the long way back from Toronto, because the countryside generally soothed her as she drove past the churches, bridges, and farmers' fields. Now nothing looked familiar and it was well past the time she had told her sister she'd be back to set up for a banquet. Her cell phone lay on the front seat next to her portfolio, which was still half open. She wasn't up to phoning home quite yet. Not with her jaw feeling as if it had been wired shut, as if she would never be able to laugh again.

I walked out of the audition, she would tell them. The problem was, she hadn't done it soon enough.

What had happened in there? How had she been so thrown off? She had gone into the fitting room. Lowered her pants halfway down her hips. Stared dumbly into the mirror, wondering if she perhaps had "thickened" too much. It had been such a force of habit to dissociate herself from her image she had stood there for God knows how long watching the insubstantial-looking blonde woman go in and out of focus. Finally, outrage had kicked in and she pulled up her pants and retrieved her portfolio from the desk. But not before she sent one of the colour copies fluttering to the floor, Steve politely turning away as she grasped about in the blinding light, finally snatching it up.

Her sister's inn was tucked behind a hill in "charming isolation" as the brochure put it. It was meant to be a way station while she and Derek, ever faithful to passive spiritual concepts, let their future unfold as it should.

"Do you fear getting older?" was the third question every interviewer asked her.

This was the one she always welcomed. The one where the full force of who she really was could shine through, tinged already with the wisdom she would surely accrue in old age.

"Not at all. I look forward to being in the autumn of my

life, being defined by who I am, rather than what I look like."

And now? A spacey montage of images bobbed through her head. Her younger, idolized self contrasted with this surprisingly shaken one.

A truth she had been circling and evading for months—perhaps even years—began to surface. Perhaps, just perhaps, she had given herself more credit than she deserved. Along with her grandmother's lips, she'd believed she had inherited her moral compass. Applying censure when life got too easy. Now she saw that the altruism she had always prided herself on might be no more than her own trumped-up aversion to being placed on a pedestal. A conceit—and she was beginning to see how big it was, she who prided herself on humility—in needing to prove that she was more than a pretty face. No great challenge in this. To speak with a modicum of intelligence was all it took to debunk the stereotype that models were thick. What a trivial goal that had been. Her world, which had seemed so global, was in the end, insular. And she saw that that the favours granted her were not for the words that came out of her mouth, but for the mouth they came out of.

She thought of her wait in Kinko's, how it was a harbinger of what lay ahead. Not being ignored so much as just unseen. What most women without remarkable looks went through every day of their lives.

The revelation embarrassed her with its obviousness, making her realize that her beauty had rendered her socially retarded, ignorant of the way the world really operated.

Not to have seen that sooner was thick, she thought now. And spotting her turnoff, she slowly headed home.

New Ground

⁓

There are streets that breathe good will. For Joanne, the ones around Ravine Park where people met daily to run their dogs had this vital quality. It was the trees, she thought; every street curving into the park was lined with elms and maples that formed an unbroken canopy. From the park, which was recessed, the effect was that of a barrier against the outside world, with the surrounding houses peeking through thick foliage.

On a Wednesday in late September, Joanne was standing in the middle of this park, looking at the houses, praying that one of them was for rent. It was a warm day, more summer than fall, sporadic reds streaking through the trees like parrot tails. Having arrived earlier than the others, she was throwing sticks for her dog, an over-exuberant black Lab who shot after every stick as if it were his last meal. While he was running she'd peer up at the houses, trying to look through the windows to see whether any rooms were empty.

Maureen will know if there's a safe place for rent, she kept telling herself. Maureen will be able to find me a nice apartment.

As if on cue (and this was encouraging, for she needed this kind of consistency in her life now), Maureen appeared at the park entrance with her white bull terrier, Jake. Something in Joanne steadied at the sight of this woman, square-jawed and auburn-haired like herself, walking down the steps in her usual attire of bulky sweater, black leggings, and belt purse around her waist filled with homemade dog biscuits. Maureen was a freelance nutritionist, and the unofficial leader of this dog group. They walked toward Joanne in their usual fashion, dog first with his stiff, debonair gait, Maureen firmly behind.

"I developed a new type of basil jelly today," Maureen said in her direct way, without preamble. "I'm trying this recipe where you use a sugar-reduced pectin."

"Oh, that sounds great," Joanne said, leaning closer to latch onto the sturdiness in Maureen's voice.

"I haven't made jelly with this kind of pectin before, so I don't know how it will taste. But I used up the last batch of basil from my garden. This year I planted six types of basil, and was really pleased with all them, except for the Thai basil, which I'm going to plant with a different kind of seed next year ..."

Joanne listened, steadying herself on images of Maureen rooting about in her garden. Even though she had heard this basil story before (and would again, for Maureen was a non-stop talker who often repeated herself and amiably invited people to interrupt her if they wanted), Joanne took everything in gratefully, as if it were physical sustenance for her ears.

"Oh. And I meant to ask you. Did Simon like the barbecue sauce for the ribs?"

Simon? Hearing her husband's name spoken aloud made Joanne feel disembodied again, and she scrambled to remember what Joanne was talking about. *The ribs. The ribs.* Oh yes—a few days ago. (A few days ago? Was it only that long ago that she had brought home the low-cholesterol barbecue sauce so Simon could try it, relieved when he showed up about ten. "The barbecue sauce that won't stick to your arteries," Joanne had chirped, in the baby-cute way she used when she sensed something explosive was coming up. He had merely grunted, gulped down the ribs, then started making more phone calls, fingers drumming the table, more frantic that she had ever seen him before.)

"Yes. He liked them. He thought they were great. I wouldn't mind buying a jar of sauce from you when you make some up again."

"I'm glad they tasted all right, because I'm always worried when I use substitute ingredients," Maureen said. "The thing about that sauce is you can use it for other things, and it's always handy to have sauces like that in the cupboard when you're both really busy." Jake put his paw out and she gave him a biscuit. "You were mentioning last week that you were both really busy at your jobs. Have things settled down for you any?"

Things were in an ugly new territory now, completely out of control. When she had suggested that it was too late to be making phone calls, Simon tore out of the house, and she had no idea where he was now. He could be on a photo shoot, he could be at a friend's house, he could be somewhere that she didn't want to know about. What she did know was that she wasn't going to go through that demeaning little exercise of phoning all his friends to find out where he was. For the past few days she had been sitting dazedly in front of her computer, doing whatever work she could, waiting for the time she could come to the park, and feel she had some sort of solid ground to stand on.

"He took on a new project ... he wants to launch a new magazine." Hearing her voice float off into hysteria, she brought it down again. "That sort of thing can be risky ... there's a lot of stress."

"Oh I can imagine," Maureen said as they watched a husky lope toward them, followed by its owners, a young married couple. "When I was working full-time, I was always under stress. I had to deal with people's personal problems, people quitting on me ..." The husky leaped on her. "Down Hank! I know you can smell fresh dog biscuits in my purse, but you mustn't jump!"

Soon there were six of them, grouped together like a human Stonehenge, while the dogs chased each other in ever-tightening circles around them. The conversation now focused on how to keep dogs from jumping up on people; Maureen was talking about how hard it had been to train Jake as a pup, how she had to work at it every day in the beginning. Joanne, who had heard this story at least ten times now, held onto every word, wanting to sink into the solidity of them.

"If you don't like the way I am, you can just fucking leave!" She could still hear Simon screaming from wherever he was right now.

Yes, well, she would be leaving all right, and this time it would be for good. But she wouldn't be chased out of her house like a woman screaming in the night, clothes being hurled out the window, neighbours watching. She would find the right place, a safe place—a place where she could feel secure while she got her thoughts and life together.

She felt her eyes once again scanning the houses overlooking the park, the ones on the street Maureen walked down every day to come here. Yes, Maureen would know of a place that was right for her in this neighbourhood. As soon as she was able to put what was happening in her life into the right words, she would ask.

* * *

Joanne had been coming to the dog park for eight months now, a little sanctuary she liked to think she had stumbled on. She never thought that such places existed, but then she never thought she'd have a dog either. That was Simon's doing, an impulse as usual, as was their moving in together, getting married on a chance trip to Vegas, starting this new magazine when he already had a hectic work schedule. When a design colleague had brought pups to work, Simon arrived home one night with a tiny black Lab that was flopping about in excitement. Claude they decided to call him, because he had such big, ungainly paws and tromped about like a clod. Having never had a puppy before, Joanne had read with bafflement the brochure that came with the puppy chow. It said puppies need consistency, calmness, and routine: regular, repetitive lessons that had to be started now. "We'll train him together! We'll do all this together!" Simon had rejoiced when she pointed out all that needed to be done. After two weeks he lost interest, and didn't even bother walking Claude in the morning anymore, so she was left with the prospect of having to exhaust a hyperkinetic, four-month-old puppy tearing through the house.

Looking back, Joanne could see it only as a time of unmitigated mania, a colossal welling up of energy that had to be dealt with, dispersed. She'd take Claude for his early morning walk, him bucking on the lead, gasping, and whipping her arm back and forth as if it were a loose branch in the wind. Later, at the computer, trying to do the technical writing she was paid to be precise at, she'd hear his choke chain bashing around downstairs. Lunch was another walk she barely had time for, supper the same thing. Ordinarily she enjoyed taking a walk, using the time to sort out her thoughts, clear her mind. But it was now just a time to fill the air with angry words: Heel! No! Down! No! Stop that! STOP THAT!!

"Can't you take the time?" she asked Simon in one of her carefully crafted voices designed to avoid further confrontations.

"No I can't! No I fucking can't! Can't you see that I'm busy?"

Well, she could see it if she wanted, but it was all too much—him barrelling home from work about eight in the evening, bolting out of bed in the middle of the night to scribble a layout, screaming down the phone at a co-worker for using the wrong colour ...

She listened to his rhapsodies, made cautionary comments, but hadn't really gleaned that he was serious about this new magazine. Mostly she just hoped it would go away. There was too much manic energy in the house now, careening through the hallways like one of those cartoon race cars that leave a spiral of rust-coloured dust in their wake. Irradiated, toxic energy that could infect other people, throttle them senseless. She wasn't even walking through the house anymore, so much as manoeuvring through it, hugging the walls along the staircase, trying to keep away from the overcharged places. Even when it was quiet, there was always a din in her ears, a low-grade screeching noise, a sensation of something speeding around a hairpin curve toward her.

* * *

Sticks, she found, tossing sticks and balls seemed to keep the puppy running, tiring him out a little. Then one afternoon when she was fitfully throwing sticks for him in the schoolyard, an older woman with two elderly white poodles came up and watched her.

"There's sort of a local dog club around here, a group of people who walk their dogs every day at five," the woman said finally.

"Oh really? Where?"

"In Ravine Park, just behind this school. You know, where you go down the steps."

Joanne tossed the ball too short as usual, causing Claude to come to an abrupt and clumsy stop.

"A park? I didn't know there was a park there."

"There are a lot of dogs for your puppy to run around with. You should join them. It will be good for you both."

* * *

The dogs were chasing each other in a clean, tight ellipse, Claude second from the lead. Having grown into his feet, he was a beautiful dog now, curves in his chest and stomach from being well exercised. For the first few weeks at the dog park, Joanne could not take her eyes off Claude, who ran and ran, his long legs flying out, the park expanding like one of those glossy magazine ads you fold out into a double page. Watching him go round and round, rapturously dispersing his excess energy, was deeply meditative. At least I'm doing this right, she'd think, focused on the dog, amazed that it was even in her to stand in one place for an hour and watch a dog play. Then she became aware of the people around her.

* * *

"Be careful when you do that with Jake," Maureen said to her husband Bill as he playfully hung the bull terrier down by his back legs and swung him back and forth. "Remember the last time you did that? He got overexcited and nipped a little kid in the arm."

Bill paused, slowed down what he was doing. His face was similar to Simon's, strong-boned and masculine, and Joanne watched in amazement as it didn't flush up, didn't twitch along the sides, didn't turn down sharply at the mouth in a threatening line. Instead, he seemed to consider what Maureen had said to him. Then, with a slightly embarrassed giggle, he set the dog back on the ground.

"Sorry, Bill," Maureen said, touching his arm. "I didn't want to play the heavy there, but I don't want Jake nipping people and then have them running around screaming that he's a vicious pit bull."

"No. That's OK. I understand."

Common courtesy between couples, Joanne thought, holding their words close. Respect. How she had come to crave the sounds of this, one of the first things she had noticed about the people here. She had entered into a territory of decent people, which was all very new to her (and impossible to describe to her old friends, who smirked at expressions like "decent people" and found her new dog fervour to be further example of her obsessive nature). But for the first time she was listening to people rather than talking, for the first time she liked people before she found out who they were, what they did.

She was so glad now that Simon hadn't come down here on weekends like she had sometimes asked him. So glad that Maureen and the others never had to listen to her voice curl up into its tense ball of caution when she told him to watch it with the dog, (or, conversely, flip into a caustic remark, the kind of whipping putdown she used to see as the hallmark of her attractiveness). Now, listening to the talk of nice, considerate people, she could see that she had not been particularly nice. Decent. "Do you two always talk to each other like that?" someone once asked when she and Simon were having a perfectly good day together. And she would think about this when she got a new place; a place where out of simple respect for herself and others, she would start making her bed, folding her clothes, take time to say hello to local shopkeepers. But first she had to find a place. Looking up at the houses peeking through the trees, she wondered again how she would ask Maureen for help in getting there.

After four days of silence, Simon had phoned (from out of town as she had suspected, on a location shoot with a photographer), and when she had said she was going to leave him, he had screamed that it was his house, his furniture, and *she* could get out now!

"You can't kick me out. I have legal rights too," she said in the tight, flat voice she used to defuse his anger. (How hateful these placating voices sounded to her now; in her new place she would be like Maureen, always using the same, self-assured tone.)

"Fuck what's legal! I don't give a fuck what's legal! Do you understand? I don't give a fuck what's legal and I want you out now!"

His voice still raced through her head like a wrecking wind and, hunched slightly so that no one could see her face, she was amazed that no one could hear it. Didn't she have the look of someone whose husband hated her right now? Couldn't they hear the endless "fuck you's" radiating through her being?

Maureen was now talking about a lamb stew she was making for supper, with potatoes from her garden. As the others joined in with accounts of their homey meals, she felt as if there were a glass partition rising to physically separate her from the rest of the group.

Such a bizarre way to live, them on one side, her on the other, but then Joanne had lived through bizarre situations before. Christmas dinner when she was thirteen. Her father hurling a turkey across the table, where it landed on a wall by the sink, flattening, sticking slightly, then sliding down, creating a crispy brown smear. Never knowing the reason for these outbursts. Getting up and leaving the table quickly so she wouldn't have to see her mother slump down to the floor in the same way.

"It's familiar," her mother had said in a resigned voice when Joanne had finally broken down and phoned her long distance that morning, asking why she had put up with her marriage for so long. "Your father and I were always fight-ing, and the sounds of fighting just became familiar to you. I'm glad you're finally leaving."

But how? She couldn't do anything in this state, with everything safe and good in the world seemingly sealed off from her. And your husband just couldn't kick you out, could he?

Maureen would know. But how would she find the right words to talk about her present situation? For she knew what Maureen's reaction would be: sympathetic, but also questioning Joanne's part in the whole mess. It takes two to tango. There are no victims, only volunteers. You knew him *how long* before you moved in? Above all, she didn't want to change her mind if Maureen did find her a place. That would be unbearable, and she would never be able to come here again. No, if she were going to ask Mau-reen for help, she had to be absolutely sure of herself. She had to stop being the woman she had been, the one who spent the night on people's couches, then laughed it off the next day; the one who frantically got friends to find her an apartment, then changed her mind; the woman who for the past four years had been littering bars and phone lines with accounts of a marriage that was always breaking up.

"You're not afraid he'll ... *do something*, are you?" her mother had asked at the end of their conversation, when she told her that Simon wanted her out now.

"If you mean beat me, no," she had answered stiffly, and probably too defensively to be believed.

As the sky darkened, everyone began leashing their dogs to go home. Joanne looked at Maureen, noting the height, hair colouring, and clothing so reassuringly similar to her own, and thought, maybe I can be like her when I "grow up." It was new for her to want to be like another woman, to actually care what that person thought. There was no way she ever wanted to put Maureen in the position of having to alter her straightforward way of speaking to ask: "Are you afraid he'll *do* ...

"I'm glad we can stop talking about lamb stew and eat it now, " Bill said dryly, making everyone laugh.

Walking Claude slowly in the opposite direction, Joanne watched as Maureen and Bill and the other couples trotted up the good streets where the good people lived. When the last of them reached the top, it was as if a draw-bridge had gone up, and her feeling of being denied entrance was complete.

* * *

"I did my accounting today," Maureen said the next day. "It took me all afternoon because I had to find forty dollars that was out."

Try being thousands of dollars out, Joanne thought, standing in her usual spot in the group, trying not to move around too much because today her head was spinning from anxiety. Try having your husband in debt to everyone, all these people phoning you, harassing you for payments of purchases you never made.

MasterCard had called today. This, with her in the middle of trying to work, trying to formulate what to say to Maureen, trying to quell the sensation that the ceiling over her head was about to fall. There had been phone calls from creditors all week, but they had been on the answering machine—remote, distant, clicked off quickly so she didn't catch any emotion in their voices. (Money? *They* needed money? How about *her*? She would need first and last month's rent with Simon in no financial position to provide it.)

When the phone rang at two that afternoon, she thought it would be one of her clients. Instead, it was a woman who introduced herself as Mrs. Bachui from MasterCard, sounding tired, desperate, and thwarted, as if she had been on a high-speed chase and had lost sight of her prey.

"I'm sorry, but he's not here. I can give you the phone number where he can be reached during the day," Joanne said with tense courtesy.

Mrs. Bachui had paused, voice genuinely hurt, shaken. "I got that number from his office and phoned him last week. He hung up on me."

He did? For a few minutes there was a shared, complicit silence as Joanne imagined this woman holding onto the receiver in the same stunned way that she did whenever Simon hung up on her. A wild, shaking anger arose at the sheer rudeness, the disrespectfulness of it all, but this was quickly replaced by the very cold fear of the realization that he seriously thought he was above the law.

"Are you his wife?" the voice said, small, hopeful.

"No." A protective lie. She wanted to scream the word "No," have huge exclamation points shooting up behind it like tree trunks. Pillars. She wanted it to echo down to the dog park and reverberate into her future. NO! NO! NO! I AM NOT HIS WIFE ANYMORE!

"I don't know what to do ..." Mrs. Bachui uttered defeatedly.

"Just keep calling him. I'm sorry he hung up on you, but

he can get ... stressed out when he's busy. The design business is very pressured." Oh, listen to her, actually defending him! But she didn't want Mrs. Bachui to think these things were so serious that she'd go after *her* money. (Was that possible? Could you leave someone, but still have his creditors coming after you? Oh, she had to talk to someone, had to find a lawyer now ...)

"When you see him again, could you tell him I called?"

"Yes, I will. And please. I apologize for him hanging up," she said, as she felt the room start to spin.

Maureen's voice now came in like a sturdy old sea rope, made tensile by wind and water. Feeling literally seasick, Joanne wanted to grab and hold onto it. But what would she say once she was pulled to shore?

She couldn't even look at Maureen now, not with eyes that for the past three years had looked at Simon's overdue bills from the tax department, credit card companies, squash clubs, men's clothing stores, chiropractors, even video stores—and then set them on the edge of his desk without saying anything, unless it was something cute: "Mr. Movie from the video store wants your money." She had diligently refused to see how much he owed, hoping it would just clear up by itself, as it always seemed to. (And oh, wasn't that a surprise that he spent money outrageously? Hadn't that been one of the attractions for her in the beginning, the thousand dollar suede jacket he had bought her, the expensive dinners, the big bushels of flowers?)

A strong wind had come up in the park, and leaves whirled around her like big, brown, flat envelopes of unpaid bills. Hunched in her static state, she felt as if they were sticking to her, as if she were being tarred and feathered.

How could you ask a person for help when you felt so unworthy? Her neck ached as if there were a ball attached to it, and she realized that, for the past hour, all she had been doing was looking at Maureen's boots: the laces, rubberized soles, and light wetness along the side. "Hanging your head in shame" the expression went, and for the first time in her life she understood its truth.

* * *

Then, as suddenly as it began, the storm was over. She had come home from buying milk last night to find Simon lying on the couch, limp, exhausted, and wearing the cowboy pyjamas she had bought him one Christmas, one button done up crookedly at the top. "Please don't leave me," he had said simply when she walked into the room. "I need you now more than ever." Now, standing in the park, her head felt slightly wobbly, as if it were a doll's head that could be yanked off and tossed to the ground.

It was an unseasonably warm, humid day. The trees surrounding the park were surrealistically bright, a hot infusion of Caribbean colours, the elms pineapple yellow, birch leaves shining like hard banana candies. Wearing T-shirts and summer shoes, everyone talked about the shock of feeling such warmth first thing in the morning. The dogs leapt higher than ever, making ecstatic lunging snaps, trying to gulp down the tropical air.

As she had expected, Simon had been under unbelievable stress over the past week, up in a helicopter most of the time, bouncing from island to island up north, trying to get vacation shots for the magazine. Crazed, it had been. Absolutely crazed, sweeping the skies with the photographer and pilot trying to find the perfect sunset, the perfect bay, the perfect cover. And yes, he was sorry, he had lost it, had been an asshole, and would apologize to everyone and straighten things out. This morning he had phoned his boss who was furious at him for missing work, and listening to Simon's voice—humorous, charming, even eloquent in its persuasion—she decided that she had overreacted. Simon did flip out when he was under stress, but the situation always resolved itself in a week or so. And it had only been a week, after all. Thinking of how she had exaggerated everything as she always did, she was angry with herself. Yes, he did scream and put people down, but most of the successful designers she knew used intimidation to draw out the best work in people. Every marriage had its rough patches. What happened to her was not so unusual.

Her mother, who had phoned to find out how things were going, wasn't so sure.

"Bad times take a lot out of you. You think when things are going well again, you can relax, but you still have to spend a lot of time getting over it."

But at least she didn't have to ask Maureen for help in getting a new place. Her relief was so great she almost toppled over from it. There was one thing though. One thing that rang in her ears that she still couldn't get out of her mind.

When they had been snuggling in bed this morning, she had said, in the baby voice she so despised, and was surprised to hear herself using again: "I don't like it when you just run out and disappear without telling me where you're going. It scares me."

"I'd do it again," he said, pinching her arm and jumping out of bed.

Something had struck her cold then—what was it? Her eyes went up to the biggest of the houses that surrounded the park, and his tone of voice came back to her. Pride. He had said he would scare her again, and he said it with pride.

* * *

"Claude seems a bit aggressive today," Maureen said as the dog broadsided Hank, the husky and pulled him to the ground.

"Yes, he's been a bit hyper lately, "Joanne said, waving a warning finger at Claude as he ran by.

"Jake gets like that too," Maureen said. "Just when you think you've got your dog trained, they go through a second adolescence. I remember that after a year with Jake, all of a sudden he became confrontational with me, and I had to start his training over ..."

Joanne listened, calming herself on this story, which she now knew by heart. It was a sodden February day, bare trees wire black from the previous night's rain. Without their leafy coverage, the houses surrounding the park had a plainer, less cozy quality. Or maybe it was her being more realistic about them, a better mindset to be making changes from. Her eyes went to the largest house and, though it could have been the bleakness of the light, she thought the top floor looked empty.

She was going ask Maureen for help in finding an apartment. Today, after the dog run, when everyone was leashing up their dogs, she was going to take Maureen aside and ask if she could talk with her privately, maybe take a walk together tomorrow morning.

"My husband and I haven't been getting along for some time ..." she would begin without preamble, getting to the point quickly to make good use of Maureen's time.

Simon was on a manic streak again, this time turning the whole house upside down. Not that there hadn't been any warning: the ballooning euphoria, frenetic planning, her feeling of being sped up around him as though he had physically attached a leash to her windpipe and was pulling her along. Renovations were his next project, although she wasn't sure he had yet cleared up his debt. On Saturday she had awoke to the sounds of banging and shoving, and when she went downstairs, she found that all the furniture from the living room had been moved into the dining room and there was a big X across one wall, which he apparently intended to knock down.

"Clean this shit up," he had said, kicking a pile of old magazines and newspapers he had thrown in a corner. She had merely looked at him, grabbed her purse, and fled to a restaurant for a long cup of coffee.

Claude made another swaggering lunge at Hank, this time sending the husky sliding across an ice patch. Dogs can pick up your vibes, Maureen often said, and, hunched in her usual position, Joanne was amazed that no one had made the connection between the dog's behaviour and her inner turmoil. Yet, she thought, Claude was overall a good dog. And when she was in her new place, hopefully not emitting jangled, toxic vibes, she would take the time to train him properly.

"If you want to leave, get the fuck out now, or I'll throw

all your things out of the house!" she could still hear Simon screaming. "I'm sick of you not fucking supporting me whenever I start a new project. I'm sick of your fucking ... betrayals!"

Now all the dogs were slipping on the ice patch, piling on top of each other, feet comically raised. Unable to join in the group's laughter, Joanne turned to the trees behind her. It was funny, but Simon's threats didn't scare her as much as they once had done. Maybe it was the months of listening to Maureen's firm, even voice, maybe it was some inner osmosis, but her voice hadn't curled up this time when she told him he couldn't throw her out because it was illegal. There was something solid in her voice now. More convincing. And when she again explained to him this morning why she had to go, she thought that, throughout all the threatening and swearing, he was actually listening to her.

He has a Jekyll and Hyde personality. We were never compatible from the start ...

The condensed, edited accounts of her marriage that she had been preparing for months, for years, went through her mind less frantically now that she knew they would be voiced aloud to Maureen. It was unfortunate that the other people in the dog group would have to know her situation, but then it would only be in the briefest form. She had never wanted these decent people to know the sordid details of her married life and, yes, it was pride on her part, defensiveness, but also respect for the healthy lives they had managed to make for themselves. Looking at the trees, which even in the dull light had a wrought iron quality, she was thankful that she had never blurted anything out here, that the tacky details of her sham marriage had never debased this hallowed ground.

"Hey. Who is that asshole driving his car into the park?" Maureen suddenly exclaimed.

Joanne turned to see Simon's car swooping into the entrance at the far end of the park. Even before Claude scooted away, she knew what was going to happen. The car door flew open, then a suitcase flew out, followed by her good coat, a pair of boots, and the bulky orange sweater she had thought was so similar to Maureen's. It fell through the air with flailing arms, and then, in an almost absurd parody of neatness, landed on the ground neatly folded.

"That's my husband. We're splitting up," she said, as his car swerved away and sped off.

Then there was pandemonium as everyone started yelling at their dogs to keep away from the clothes. Something went off in her, plunging her into formless white light. But she felt her feet on the ground, pressure on her arm, and Maureen's body against hers, moving her forward.

Salvation

"**D**raw me next!"

Donna looked up at the scrawny, 12-year-old girl glowering at her from the other end of the classroom table. She was just finishing a drawing of Matthew, another student, and paused in her shading.

"Our deal was that you'd finish your homework first, Christina. Remember?"

Christina shoved a half-completed math assignment into her backpack, then flung it onto the floor with enough force to send it skidding.

"I *am* finished!"

Donna strove to project the calm, matter-of-fact manner recommended in the volunteer manual for Just Cause, Toronto's longest running centre for children with behavioural problems. Housed in a converted mansion in the working class Dundas Street area, it offered anger management programs and, every Wednesday after school, The Homework Club. Tacked to the walls were assignments on how children dealt with their feelings of anger. One posed the dilemma: "What do you do when your best friend calls you stupid?" with Donna's all-time favourite answer being: "I sware, Kick the wall, Go to my room to try and *clam* down." From outside came the cries of children playing on the basketball court. She looked evenly at the girl whose unremittingly plain features she now knew by heart, and said: "Your mother told me you had to study your multiplication. So how about you do that, and the rest of your work, and then I'll draw you?"

Ignoring this, Christina stalked over to a shelf of board games. Donna turned her attention back to Matthew, who was self-consciously posing for his portrait, his reward for completing an essay on Harry Potter. With his bulldog jaw and pug nose, he had the dim-witted look of a James Cagney thug, which was misleading, because he was the smartest student in the class. Minimizing his jawline with a few deft strokes, she then subtly lengthened his eyelashes, giving them a more poetic cast.

June sunlight streamed through the windows, reminding Donna that her tutoring stint would soon be coming to an end. The six months at the Homework Club had gone by fast, too fast, as the unexpected highlight of her week in what was otherwise an upsetting time. She had lost her job as an executive producer at the cable station she had helped set up. No other job offers were coming in. Up until now, Donna hadn't been much of a "do-gooder," preoccupied as she was with doing good for herself. But driving home one afternoon after a lunch date that was cancelled at the last minute, dreading having to face her silent condo, she came across a billboard for Just Cause. "Take away the bully before it takes away a childhood," it read. And long-divorced, childless, heading into her fifties, she found herself phoning to volunteer.

"Forget about turning these kids into scholars," she had joked to friends after the first few sessions. "Just getting them to sit still for 15 minutes is a major achievement."

Even that seemed too ambitious a goal with the end of the school year approaching. The idea of drawing portraits had occurred to her when she realized that bargaining, and doling out the mandatory lavish praise for substandard work could no longer keep them motivated. She had been a good artist when she was young, growing up as a nomadic military brat, always the new kid in class. To get friends, she would draw flattering likenesses of the kids she wanted to hang out with in the margins of her notebook, which never failed to ingratiate her to them. Would it work for this group, she had wondered, when Matthew had flat-out refused to study his spelling a couple of weeks before? She started sketching him, gratified when it captured, then held, his easily fractured attention. When he asked to bring the drawing home, she said it was conditional on him spelling ten new words.

Now she had an audience of sorts grouped around her: Scott, the other tutor, a handsome, 25-year-old computer analyst, and Kaitlin and Destiny, two cute girls she had drawn the previous week. Not liking to be left out, Christina returned to the table and slipped her math homework out of her backpack, making a motion, at least, to consider the offer. Donna didn't push it. If Matthew's thuggish features belied his intelligence, Christina's pointy face accurately reflected her unbounded hostility. Even an innocuous question like "How was school today?" could elicit a withering glare that had the capacity to utterly cow Donna. The most odious child she had ever met in her life, she thought.

She softened when she began reading about learning

problems. Much of Christina's anger stemmed from being three grades behind her age level, with most questions about school a goading reminder of some failure, academic or social. Donna persisted, stumbling upon some formula of firmness and playful coercion that lowered Christina's defences and even garnered, one week, a surprise hug. That tiny victory was short-lived. The following week—right in front of Scott and the other students—Christina had snarled: "You're not *cool* enough to be my tutor."

Bright coins of fuchsia had flared up on Donna's cheeks. Very bad timing, this remark, for she had recently come up hard against the wall of age discrimination in the television business. Recruiters mentioning younger demographics, saying they were looking for someone with "a little *less* experience." And now this, ageism in volunteer work! "Do you think that's a nice thing to say?" was the centre's recommended response to a child's insult. But fed up with the whole world at that moment, beyond caring if she got "fired" from this stint, Donna had looked Christina squarely in the eye and said: "Get over it, kid."

Whether this had even sunk in, Donna couldn't tell, but she was relieved to see Christina now buckling over an equation. She began shading in Matthew's forehead, grateful that Scott, who occupied the highest rung of coolness as far as the kids were concerned, was still leaning over her shoulder, watching her.

"You're good. Did you ever take art classes?" he asked.

"No, but I used to draw cartoons in class."

Cartoons? Was that how she referred to that vile comic strip she had created when she was 13, a shameful memory of a boy mouse that unexpectedly popped to mind the other day while she was sending another resume off into cyber-space?

Matthew began to squirm, distracted by the cries from the basketball court. "I saw this guy at the Ex last summer, drawing people? And he drew them really fast? But you draw faster."

Donna smiled with false humility, thinking that that guy only had seconds to study his subjects, whereas she had painstakingly memorized her students' features so that it would look like the sketches rolled off the tip of her pencil. She glanced at Christina who was now frowning at an equation, never a good sign. "How are you coming along there?" she asked.

"Quit bothering me."

Donna let this go, noticing that Christina was strug-gling over six times three, which they had gone over count-less times. What would that feel like, to try and try and try, and have nothing stick? What did Christina do when she was called stupid—more likely *stoooooopid*—God knows how many times in the course of a day? Did she "sware, kick the wall, go her room to try to *clam* down?"

"Three times six. Three times six," Christina muttered under her breath.

"What's five times three? Add another three," Scott prompted.

Sensing that this too, was beyond Christina, Matthew said kindly: "It's eighteen."

"Oh yeah," she said, quickly writing it down.

With a show-offy flourish, Donna finished her drawing.

"Hey dude, it looks like you!" Scott said. Glancing at his enhanced likeness with considerably more indifference than he had shown the previous week, Matthew shoved the paper into his backpack.

"Cool. Can I go out now?"

Donna nodded, disappointed, for she had high hopes for him. She had imagined him wanting to continue their lessons throughout the summer; he would read more novels, enlarge his vocabulary, go on to win national spelling bees, all of which she would capture in an award-winning documentary.

When he galloped out of the classroom, followed by Kaitlin and Destiny, who didn't even ask for a portrait, she felt a surge of panic. Scott would follow, then of course, Christina, leaving her all alone in the room. But no, Scott hung in, and helped Christina struggle through the rest of the equations.

"I'm finished!" she announced, crunching the page into her backpack.

"Do you have any other homework?" Donna asked.

"An essay, but I'm not going to do it."

"Why not?"

"Because I'm *not*!"

"Well, wasn't that our deal? That you'd finish all of your homework and then I'd do a drawing of you?"

"I'm not going to *do* it!"

Christina's face closed into a defiant homeliness that would curtail her already limited opportunities as an adult. She stood on the threshold, Donna thought, of either moving forward or being stranded in special-ed, sheltered and unprepared for the real world. Donna wouldn't do her any favours by caving in now. But given her recent run of rejections she lacked the fortitude to risk even a minor failure.

"Do you want me to draw you?"

"I don't care."

"Tell you what then," Donna said, getting a blank piece of paper. "Why don't you look straight at me and lower your head a bit?"

She began with an outline of the face, softening the chin slightly. Christina watched with the wary eyes of someone used to being led into ridicule (and oh, how easy it would be to do a cruel caricature, emphasize the rat-like cast of her features, throw on mouse ears, a tiny tail for good measure). Of all the portraits, Donna had prepared for Christina's the most. It would be insulting to make her look falsely pretty, but she could tweak the sides of her lips to bring out an inherent impishness. Make Christina look like a cute kid. The kind of kid who, when her face wasn't hardened in vigilance against the unending litany of *stoooopids*, could actually be nice to be with.

She glanced at the anger management assignments on the walls. Few of these children, as ill-tempered as they might sometimes be, were true bullies in the sense of calculating and exploiting a victim's weakness. Their learning problems segregated them, made them victims themselves. One poster, tacked to the bulletin board, described the various forms of bullying: hitting, shoving, name-calling, teasing, and shunning. She looked back at her pencil, so harmless, but in the right hands, so powerful, and her recent, repugnant memory of her 13-year-old self flooded back to her. Drawing. No one had ever mentioned drawing as a way of bullying.

* * *

Her comic strip, "The Adventures of Martin Mouse, Tales of Uncommon Strength and Valour," was conceived in a boring grade-eight math class. Whatever possessed her to make Martin Burke, a short, unprepossessing classmate with oversized glasses who had never done anything to annoy her the mock hero of her story, she couldn't say. Very likely, her initial drawing of him in a superhero costume, with a tail, mouse ears, jutting ribs and fake biceps, drew a smirk from one of the popular girls—all the encouragement she needed. What amazes her is that she had almost completely forgotten about it until a few days ago. Was it all the mental minimizing of pug noses and pointy chins that had sparked the memory?

A hero needs a damsel in distress, and she had chosen the most obese girl in school, whom she christened "The Blob." Plot lines usually involved The Blob getting stuck in a doorway or phone booth, and crying "Save me! Save me, Martin Mouse!" Rushing to her defence, Martin would encounter more humiliations: tripping over his tail, his fake biceps slipping down his arms, huffing and puffing with all his might, but still too weak to rescue The Blob. By the end of the story he would be crying: "Save me! Save me! It's Martin Mouse!"

She is so grateful now that photocopiers or the Internet didn't exist back then, so the strip was only distributed in the classroom. The teacher, meek, effeminate Mr. Finnegan, never dared reprimand her beyond mild disapproval. A crush on a guy who liked demure girls made her give up the strip eventually. As it was, Martin's adventures had begun to lose their novelty among her classmates, making her work all the harder to come up with more outrageous episodes. Martin having sex with The Blob, who, unable to feel his mite-sized penis, simply shoved him whole up her cavernous vagina where he remained stuck for three or four more panels, his tail sticking out of her like a tampon string. His sperm proved mighty, for he ended up impregnating her with sextuplets: blob-like circles that she embellished with glasses, tiny mouse ears and tails; they were all mentally challenged, misspelling words like cat, doomed to be in grade three forever.

* * *

Christina's nose, with its broad tip, was now giving her trouble. Erasing it, she tried again, breaking the spell of artistic effortlessness. Scott got up to watch the basketball game; Christina instantly swivelled in his direction.

"Christina. Could you face me for one second longer? Just one second?"

Christina complied for exactly one second, then bounded over to Scott.

"Can I go out to play now?"

"Sure Chris. But don't you want Donna to finish your portrait first?"

Donna shifted the paper so that Christina could see that it was the most flattering depiction of herself that she would ever have in her life. And in a flash she understood that it meant nothing to the girl. Any parent would have regarded this disinterest as trivial on a sunny summer day (from a child with an attention deficit disorder yet!). But Donna wasn't a parent, or a producer, or a boss, or a wife, or any of those women's roles that came with a purpose or a perspective. If Christina was at a threshold, so was she; either Donna would emerge stronger from her recent setbacks or be forever weakened by them. She had, through the course of her career, managed celebrities, CEOs, and politicians. Who would have thought that it could all boil down to this, her self-esteem irrationally contingent on one irascible little girl who might not even make it to the seventh grade?

She tried again.

"Christina. Don't you want this?"

It came out like a plea, the very essence of neediness. And what Christina did diminished her even more than a flat-out no. She skipped out of the room as if Donna were so inconsequential as to have never existed at all. It was the perfect slap in the face, and Donna wanted to laugh or cry at the long-delayed, well-deserved comeuppance of it all, going from the chosen to the devalued.

She dashed off Christina's grinning mouth, hating the way Scott had seen her cheeks burning with embarrassment.

"I guess I'll go outside now," he said, glancing around the empty room. "I don't think there's anything else to do here."

"No."

Alone in the classroom, she began clearing the table. Martin's cartoon face, with its grim forbearance, the hurt in his eyes that she could see even now she had managed to capture on paper back then, loomed before her. Nothing hurt more than name-calling, they said in the workshops. That wasn't true. Being labelled stupid, hurtful as it was, might at least bond you to a group, even if it was under-achieving. A drawing—with its dead-on depiction of your unique physical and psychological weaknesses—exerted far more damage. Small comfort now, to concoct happy outcomes for Martin and that poor, unknown girl she had christened The Blob, envisioning them with happy families and secure jobs with pensions.

And were they able to draw her now, what would their drawing be?

An aging, single woman, once considered glamorous, running out of options. Her hair would be too long for her age, her skirt a bit too short, and her arms would be outstretched, parasitically seeking praise under the guise of altruism. Ahead of her, a never-anticipated plateau of vulnerability and insignificance. And as for the words issuing from the voice balloon above her head, she could see them too. "Help me! Help me!" she would cry to the scornful children who were fleeing her. "Save me."

The Girl Next Door

⟿

The phone rang. Marina was sure it would be one of her clients phoning to cancel. Breathe, she told herself, feeling the cleansing breath she'd spent years perfecting catch midway in her chest and ricochet back into her throat. The phone sat on the ledge of her living room window, the venetian blinds tightly drawn. Letting it ring a second time, she prepared herself for what the client—no doubt that V.P. at the pharmaceutical company—would say. "How are you?" the V.P. would begin, her tone all sugary with curiosity. Then, after the requisite small talk, she would just come out with it. "Was that *you* I saw on the news last night? Do you *live* there?"

Instead, it was the secretary from Grace's school saying that Grace wanted to speak with her.

"Grace! Are you all right, honey?"

"I'm OK ... but my stomach hurts."

"It does honey? Does it hurt a little bit or a whole bunch?"

This reversion to baby talk with her ten-year-old daughter was a compensatory habit Marina had fallen into lately. According to the teacher, several of her classmates had called home lately, complaining of stomach pains and headaches—the usual bodily response to a traumatic event that was too much to assimilate—but this was the first time for Grace. She seemed to be coping almost too well.

"I don't know ... it doesn't hurt too bad, I guess ..."

"Do you want me to come and pick you up now?"

Another jagged breath nicked Marina's chest wall as a siren screeched on the street below. "Grace? Are you still there? Do you want me to pick you up now?"

"Um ... I don't know, because the teacher said this afternoon we're going over stuff for our test."

"So do you think you feel well enough to stay, or do you want me to come and get you?

Another long pause. Grace's usual indecision had intensified lately. Marina edged closer to the shaded window, wondering how many reporters were out there, cozying up to the locals. Letting the whole world know about her neighbourhood. "Shabby Victorian row houses divided into rentals on a street full of colourful characters," was how one newspaper put it, her unit prominently displayed in the accompanying photo.

"Maybe after school would be better."

"OK then. I'll see you at a quarter to four, sweetie. I'll pick you up right outside your classroom. *Love* you."

She hung up, her skin prickling from the stuffy heat in her darkened apartment. Bright June sunlight pressed against the slats of her blinds, as if any second now it might crash through like surf. You've got to get out of here, she thought. Go to Dufferin Mall, maybe pick up some Tums for Grace. Halfway down the hall to get her keys, she remembered she couldn't leave or enter her house without enduring more police questioning. They had been courteous enough at first. But now with more evidence being uncovered, they'd started treating everyone on the block as if they were accomplices in their collective, utter oblivion as to what had occurred in front of their eyes in broad daylight.

Why was *this* happening just when things were finally coming together for her? Divorce almost dealt with; goals set. Trust that the universe, her unreliable friend, would finally help her expand into the fullest potential of what she was meant to be. No clients had cancelled yet. Which meant that there was still a good chance that she would be holding a weekend retreat called "Accessing Intuition Through Yoga" for 24 women executives at the Muskoka Sands Inn, the most exclusive location she had ever booked for an event.

Another sound made her neck jerk upright. The whispered scraping of some steely tool. Tweezers clicking on a hard surface—a kitchen floor—or a countertop maybe. Could it be the investigators picking up a trace of something?

No. She couldn't possibly hear anything happening in *that* apartment. Several walls—thick, well-built brick walls—separated them.

She stared at her course notes sprawled out on her coffee table, spouting what now seemed absurdities about the inviolable power of a woman's intuition. What was worse? Being trapped here? Or undergoing another interrogation by that arrogant cop stationed at her front door?

What is your name?

Do you own or rent your home?

How long have you been living at this address?

Too long.

* * *

When she first saw the police helicopter, weeks ago, so high in the sky, scanning the ten-block area of investigation like some prehistoric bird, she felt odd bursts of comfort under her terror. Whoever did that to the little girl—the person or persons still out there—must know that they were being watched, even though, realistically, the helicopter had no way of spotting them, from so far above the real world. With the crime also came the news—repeated in every newspaper article and TV and radio broadcast—that the greatest percentage of the city's sex offenders were concentrated in her area.

No surprise there. She wanted to move to a better area. She knew from her criminology courses that a sex offender, once his crime became known, was likely to strike again before getting caught. During the unbearable month the killer remained loose, the police made a desperate appeal to area residents, urging them to search their memories for small clues about anything that might have been out of the ordinary that day, anyone who looked suspicious.

Was it you, she'd wonder about a stocky, balding, too genial-looking guy strolling down Dundas Street with his head thrust back as if determined to whistle a happy tune. Or you, she'd wonder at the tatty-haired, lost soul who regularly paced the steps of the local mall, wearing the same Toronto Maple Leafs hockey shirt day-in, day-out. Years of yoga training had given her a heightened sensitivity to the body's messages. She scanned people's backs, the set of their shoulders, their hands, for any sign of the monstrous finesse that could butcher a young girl's body into eight pieces, with a pleading hope that her intuition would announce the killer's identity with a resounding "*There!*"

And then, there it was. Driving Grace home from school one afternoon, she saw, hovering over her home, the familiar police helicopter, suspended in a foreboding stillness, no longer searching.

He had done it mercifully fast, in his apartment two doors down from hers. Not the predictable sex offender type after all, but a computer analyst without a criminal record, who worked for the government. She was not lying —to the police, her friends, her family, or more importantly, even to herself, when she said that she had never seen the guy. God knows, if she had seen him, a nondescript, preppy-looking man swinging a briefcase, she would have thought that his very middle-class innocuousness added respectability to the neighbourhood.

The phone rang, making her jump. The secretary at Grace's school again; apparently she had changed her mind and wanted Marina to come and take her home.

"OK, honey. I'll come and get you."

The first thing she saw when opening her front door to the glare of sunlight was the police barricade. Not the usual flimsy yellow tape they used on cop shows, but one made of permanent-looking metal: a waist-high fence sealing off the sidewalk in front of her house, from one block to the other. Pausing just outside her front door, she took in the crowd. Twice as many people as this morning, bonded by the inflated and fleeting camaraderie that a brutal crime provides. Arnie, the sleazy owner of the local video store, all spruced up in a suit jacket, chatting up a TV cameraman; her main floor tenant Wanda—already three sheets to the wind by the looks of it, rubbing elbows with the forlorn looking guy in the Toronto Maple Leafs hockey shirt. Everywhere, the police directed traffic; the stream of drivers slowing down to gawk, the pedestrians being herded to the other side of the street. And presiding over his domain on the segregated stretch of sidewalk, the same cocky policeman she had dealt with earlier this morning.

He was tall and blonde, his shoulders a smug wall of authority. Hundreds of eyes fastened on her as she walked down the porch steps trying to project an aura of professionalism. An educated woman. The only person in her Portuguese family to have graduated from university (with honours yet, while coping with a baby and a collapsing marriage!). Someone who still hoped to get her Masters in clinical psychology one day.

"Name?" the policeman asked.

Her lips hitched up in a tight, beatific smile. The guy had been caught.

Why were they still interrogating her? Out of the corner of her eye, she caught Wanda waving at her, and pretended not to see.

"Officer, you know who I am. We went through this earlier this morning when I took my daughter to school. Remember?"

He indicated a spot to the side of her porch, almost directly in front of a cameraman perched on the other side of the barricade. "Could you step over there, please? And could I see two pieces of ID?"

She fumbled through her wallet, knowing he was grandstanding for the pretty young reporter who had tried to interview her the other day, and who now inched toward them, motioning to her cameraman.

"I'm Marina Marquez. I own this place. I have to pick up my daughter from school. She's really sick."

The policeman scrutinized her driver's licence with the same show of officious intensity he had used earlier that morning, dragging it out so that the reporter could get the camera in position. Marina ducked, noticing for the first time how her porch sloped up at the side almost in a caricature of lower-class shabbiness.

"Look, I have to pick up my daughter," she said, advancing a step. A mistake, for the policeman physically blocked her with his chest. This is what will be on the news tonight, she thought, her nose almost pressed to his sternum. This is what your clients will see. You, among the colourful riffraff of your street, being treated like some slumlord.

* * *

A dream is a goal with a plan and a deadline. A quote she had inscribed on a Post-it Note last spring, and stuck on her bathroom mirror. Putting her place up for sale this month was her top priority. She and Grace had drawn up a list of what they wanted most.

No tenants, just us, was Grace's biggest wish. A huge financial adjustment to be made there, for Marina's main floor and basement tenants covered the bulk of her mortgage. Her father had bought the unit for her for practically nothing when she had returned from her year of studying yoga in India, pregnant, with her new husband Stefan in tow. Accustomed to the poverty of Asia, the shabbiness of the neighbourhood barely registered at first. When she got her graduate degree, when Stefan, brilliant but direction-less, figured out what he wanted to do with his life, they would think about moving.

Though the city's real estate market had soared, her area had stayed flagrantly flat. She had been waiting for it to evolve from an "area in transition" to at least decently lower middle class. And now, this happening.

* * *

Howard, her basement tenant, emerged from his apartment into the sunlight like a stooped blinking mole, diverting the policeman's attention away from her, so she could get to her car. The forensic team was still combing the back alley where she usually parked, so the city had given her a park-ing permit for a side street two blocks away. Head down, she ploughed past the crowd toward her ancient, beat-up Volvo. Once in the car, she turned onto Lansdowne, the street where the girl had last been seen.

Lush, mature oaks lined the street, but Marina saw them as ominous now, knowing that their beauty that spring had lulled a young girl into a false sense of safety, particularly after one of the coldest winters in a decade. Hadn't Marina—who yes, in answer to *that* question, *was* home that day—felt optimistic with the warmer weather too? Almost unreasonably so, with her goals set, a new sense of purpose? In the long-awaited sunshine of that May day, it would have been easy for a responsible ten-year-old to convince her mother to let her walk five minutes to a friend's place by herself. Hadn't Grace been begging to go out alone ever since she turned ten?

Every parent grappled with this issue, but Marina hated refusing Grace opportunities to develop her independence—especially since Grace had the maturity that children of struggling mothers often develop, rarely asking Marina for anything more than she could give.

She had finally relented this spring, allowing Grace to cross the street to the corner store by herself, but only if Marina watched her the entire time. A secret pleasure anyway, for Grace was growing into a beauty, the kind of girl people described as "wholesome," "refined," and "girl next door." From her vantage point at the living room window, she would watch Grace run, pumping the long legs she had inherited from her father's Swiss side of the family, with her straight, honey-blonde hair flying out behind her. The store was a black hole of a sell-everything junk heap. Into its gloom Grace would vanish, and after a few interminable minutes would emerge, look both ways, and dash across the street with as much comic dignity as her new, truncated independence allowed. Now, nearing Grace's school, Marina had a sickening thought that she immediately suppressed: did *he* ever stand at his living room window, with the same second floor vantage point, and watch too?

The visitor's parking lot behind the school lay empty. She parked, relieved that Grace had asked to be picked up early, thereby avoiding any encounter with other parents. A week ago, she had felt a camaraderie with them; terrified parents staunching their feelings to put up a charade of normalcy for the sake of their children. But now, with everyone knowing about her proximity to the event ...

She expected to find Grace waiting in the office, but it was empty save for the school secretary, Lydia. She immediately looked up from her desk.

"Marina! How are you?"

"Gooooood. Is Grace here?"

"She'll be down in a minute," Lydia said brightly. Then: "Are the investigators still at your place?"

"They are."

"Have they found anything yet?"

How the fuck should I know? Marina wanted to say. Do you think I actually go to that apartment, knock on the door, and ask the forensic group what they've come up with? A bone shard? A strand of hair?

"I don't know. I've been so busy with work lately. I'm leading a retreat at Muskoka in two weeks." This barely registered with Lydia, who simply nodded as if Marina were a child making things up. "And I don't want to know. I'm not watching the news anymore, reading anything about it ..."

Lydia shook her head and shuddered. "I don't blame you. If I lived next door to *him* ..."

"We don't live next door! We live two doors down!"

Just then, Grace walked in, looking smaller than she had this morning, dwarfed by her pink Barbie backpack, which was slipping off one shoulder. Conscious of the cameras, Marina had insisted—without an argument from Grace—that she dress in her good clothes today: an embroidered denim skirt and fitted Gap T-shirt. But the hem of her skirt slanted crookedly above one knee, giving her a neglected, ragamuffin look.

"All set?"

Grace nodded an indeterminate yes or no, not looking at her. Ordinarily, Marina would have enclosed her in a big hug, but the constant scrutiny had made them self-conscious around each other in public, and they stood apart in stilted silence while Grace was signed out.

The sunlight was sharper now, delineating the dents in her Volvo. A month ago, her major concern was how she was going to pull up in front of the Muskoka Sands Inn in this piece of shit without any of her clients spotting her. Yoga teachers weren't supposed to be wealthy, but she didn't want her clients—especially this well-heeled group—to know how financially precarious her life was, how she occasionally worked as a blackjack dealer at her brother's casino in Hamilton to make ends meet. Now the car provided the sealed-off sanctuary that she was grateful for.

Grace sunk into the passenger seat, and propped her feet up on her backpack.

"What kind of homework do you have?"

"Just geography."

"Oh, that shouldn't be so bad." Grace's teacher was big on colouring maps, which Marina loved helping her with. Look, she'd say, pointing to the countries in central and southeast Asia. I've been there, I've been there, and I swam in the Indian Ocean. With sharks once!

"Weren't you scared?" Grace had asked.

"A little," Marina had replied.

"What are you most afraid of now?"

Losing you. Always, always losing you. She now ran her fingers through Grace's hair, a compulsive gesture, needing to touch her to convince herself that she was still there. "I thought it might be fun to get a video."

"OK." Her brow furrowed as Marina turned onto an unfamiliar street. "Aren't we going to Arnie's video store?"

Not since he gave that interview to the paper, the very last article Marina had read on the subject. Swollen with his temporary stardom, he had rhapsodized about the accused's surprisingly eclectic taste in movies; predictably, *The John Gacy Story*, but also the unexpected *Josie and the Pussycats*, which he had apparently rented before Marina. Even thinking that she had touched something he had touched, maybe picked up one of his skin cells ...

"I thought we could go to the one on Keele. They have a better selection. Does that sound all right to you?"

"OK."

"Do you want to listen to Katy Perry?"

"OK."

Marina rummaged about in the back seat, sending a tower of tranquillity tapes clattering against a pile of her latest promotional brochure. Her style of yoga—which she laboured over to explain without sounding flaky—accessed the deep feminine wisdom of the body. Wisdom beyond mere mind, as she planned to say at the workshop. Wisdom that was pure instinct and accessible through breath.

Sliding in the CD, she thought of the other parents in the city who were breathing a collective sigh of relief that the guy had been caught. A release of breath too powerful to be taught in a yoga class, one starting deep in the pelvis and drawing upwards, releasing all the terror stoked since reading the headline—"Have you seen this girl?" A breath that would end in an explosion of giddy laughter if you didn't think of the girl's parents.

Grace crooned along with Katy, her voice in tune with

the lower notes. She looked tired, but she was sleeping well. Unnaturally well, probably, but that was a function of her dissociation. What would Marina do when Grace woke up from the inevitable nightmare of a butcher knife slashing through her bedroom wall?

Once, when Grace was four, she had awoken crying in the middle of the night. "Why do there have to be bad people in the world?" Stefan had surprised Marina by rousing himself out of his burgeoning apathy to sit up with Grace, and comfort her. How would he counsel her now, she wondered, as she turned onto one of the nicer streets along High Park. The geographically absent father, remarried and living in Zurich, apparently content to see his beautiful daughter once a year.

The houses on this street had an empty look, no cars in the driveways, no pedestrians. The quiet seemed to congeal in every veranda, amplifying their space, making them great basins of privacy.

"Oh look!" Grace cried. "There's a house for us!"

It took Marina a moment to realize she was pointing at a small bungalow on the corner with a "For Sale" sign in front. Oh yes, the house-choosing game they had been playing for the past three months. She slowed down and took in the putty-coloured clapboard and the smart white trim.

"You think the lawn is big enough?" she asked.

"It looks OK."

"But it doesn't have a tree out front. Remember? We wanted a tree out front?"

"That's OK ... I don't need one."

She heard the unhappy, suppressed longing in her daughter's voice.

"Here," she said, handing Grace one of her brochures from the back seat. "Write down the real estate agent's number on this and we'll look at it on the weekend."

When they entered the video store on Keele, Marina's breath almost stopped. The John Gacy videos—with a vile close-up of his face—were lined up on the front shelf next to copies of *Josie and the Pussycats*. Was this for real? Had one of the clerks—a guy no doubt, some sad, sick, Quentin Tarantino wannabe—read the newspaper article about the accused's taste in movies and decided that it would hilarious to replicate it here?

That interview with Arnie, the interview she had read despite her misgivings, swam back to her mind with sickening clarity. How the accused had kept *Josie and the Pussycats* out for two weeks, and good-naturedly paid the late charges. Little girls in that movie. Little girls in tiny tops and tiny skirts squealing over the big girl band. Barrelling toward the clerk—a dull-looking teenage girl behind the counter—she suddenly became aware of a space behind her, a chilling absence.

"Grace? ... Did you see my daughter?"

The clerk shook her head dumbly, just as Marina did when the police showed her the missing girl's photo.

"Grace! Where are you?"

The fluorescent lighting was disorienting. *There were no instincts as fine-tuned as that of a predator.* Swinging into the comedy aisle, she sent several copies of *Porky's* crashing to the floor, then grabbed the wide-eyed girl clutching a Barbie video.

"Didn't I tell you to stay with me? Did I tell you *never* to leave my sight?"

Grace's lower lip trembled. And Marina's damned up tears began to flow.

"I'm sorry I yelled at you, Grace."

"That's OK."

"Do you want to go home now?"

"OK."

* * *

The crowd in front of her place had increased, a vast pilgrimage of spectators that kept coming and coming. Together as a unit, they walked down the segregated stretch of sidewalk, which the blonde policeman still commandeered.

"Name?" he asked.

"You know it, officer. Why don't you tell me?"

His jaw tensed in anger. Why couldn't she keep her head up? Why was it now like a lead ball, rolling toward her front porch?

Oh, the things she didn't want to know, the details she wished she had never found out. At five-thirty, he had dragged the girl to the alleyway behind Marina's house, which her kitchen window overlooked. The window she'd probably been standing in front of, slicing red peppers for a salad, that wise, inner voice she harped on about, never once telling her to look up.

"Sorry, sorry, sorry," she started mumbling to someone, not the officer, who nonetheless interpreted it as an apology.

"You can go in," he said, and she felt Grace's hand on hers, leading her up the steps.

* * *

"Accessing Intuition Through Yoga" went surprisingly well—two days of towering clouds and azure water affording a suitably transcendent setting for the women executives who had paid good money for the retreat at the Muskoka Sands Inn. Spiritually stripped, Marina's body did all the things her mind could not. Smiled. Kept her shoulders straight. Laid her hands on necks and backs, giving the impression that she could feel muscular blocks, when the truth was that there was very little she could feel these days. Yet when the course concluded on Sunday afternoon, everyone clapped with the kind of heartfelt appreciation she had once craved.

Driving home, Marina was aware of the rising and falling of her diaphragm, taking her first deep inhalations in weeks. Just before the toll route, she pulled up beside a small lake and stared at the water.

Insight, she had told her class, is literally that, a sight within, seeing into another mindset as if you had a window on another world. Gazing at the water, a particular window appeared—*his* window. She saw that during those spring days when she had allowed Grace her abbreviated sprints across the street that he had been watching too, from his own apartment two doors down. Marina saw now that Grace had been his first choice. Wholesome. Refined. Within reach. But—and he had *known* this—protected. They had stood at their windows, almost side by side, murderer and mother, the two of them bound by the spell of pure, shared love, unable to take their eyes off Grace as she took her first mad dash to the woman she would someday be.

Memory Loss

⁓

Everyone agreed. Neil had become so much nicer since his accident. In fact, it was almost a blessing in disguise the way everything had turned out, wasn't it?

Most days—albeit tentatively, not wanting to tempt fate—Carol agreed. But sitting around the picnic table by the lake, the sun setting after a euphorically normal day at the cottage, she became alert to a lingering repercussion: Neil starting to stumble over a story he was telling Bob about his early days as a food photographer.

"So, the client kept saying, this soup doesn't look *chunky* enough ..." he chortled, then abruptly stopped.

A breeze set the water shuddering pink. Tensing, Carol tried to gauge the timbre of the pause. Was he stuck? Or merely thinking? On the deck, their nine-year-old son Daniel was setting up a haul of water balloons with Bob's son Max. He glanced sharply at his father, then looked away.

"So, ah ... ah, what we did ... what happened was ..."

Neil blinked in benign bewilderment. Carol sensed the drop in memory as if he were a trapeze artist who had missed his catch and was falling into space. Bob, his racing buddy, who was with him the day of the accident, grinned as if the hesitation were merely a set up for a punchline. Deftly Carol jumped in.

"You put marbles in the soup," she prompted.

"Oh yeah! We put marbles in the soup. We mixed these marbles in with the vegetables."

"And then you had them colour-corrected to look like carrots."

"We spent the whole night making those goddam marbles look like carrots. And then when the client saw the photo, he said: 'Now this soup really looks like chunky vegetable!'"

Everyone laughed naturally; it was not at all forced. If Daniel was embarrassed by his father's falter, he wasn't showing it; his attention was fully on the upcoming water balloon fight. Gratitude welled up, tempered by the guilt that was always provoked by reminders of the accident. Could she have caused it? The question seemed remote, like music heard from a boat across a lake—a chord recognized, then gone. With a wild whoop, Daniel leapt into the air to dodge the balloon Max had thrown at his head. Something pinched her wrist, and she realized that she was doing it, squeezing Neil's hand so tightly that her knuckles had almost whitened.

* * *

A year ago she wouldn't have been having this kind of weekend. A single mother who just happened to be married was how she described herself, although "racetrack widow" was more accurate. As long as she had been with Neil, virtually every summer weekend was booked for racing motorcycles. Daytona. Road America. Shannonville. All the grubby little tracks around greasy little towns where race fanatics congregated in trailers, pick-ups, and vans. Even hearing the names of the tracks could make Carol feel dismissed like a June bug being clipped on a side-view mirror. And she could see herself watching Neil loading his precious Ducati onto his truck, while Daniel, who would once again be spending the weekend alone with her, looked on.

"Why do you let him race?" every woman, even if she had just met Carol, deemed it her business to ask.

"If he wants to kill himself, that's his problem," was her stock reply.

"What about your son?"

Carol had no prepared answer for this. She was still stunned with anger that Neil had continued to race after Daniel was born. It made her feel chronically off-centre, as if she had just dodged a blow and was frozen in position. Yet it was anger she could usually contain, keep from spilling into her everyday life.

Besides, that life, for the most part, suited her. For all his recklessness, Neil was a good provider, constantly seeking new ways to expand his business. Racing was even a release from it all, he claimed; the worrying about whether he would be able to make his studio costs, and compete with the hordes of up-and-coming photographers out to steal his clients. They had agreed that she would give up her career as a real estate agent once they had children. But an emergency hysterectomy three years after Daniel was born ended all dreams of a large family.

One child. The archaic luxury of looking after only *one*

child, full time. To dispel any notions that she was a pampered hausfrau, Carol helped out at a soup kitchen, took courses to complete her degree in art history, and made herself ridiculously available to ferry around the children of busier moms. Still, the feeling of being judged persisted, as if there were a jury of black-robed women permanently installed in her head.

Why do you let him race?

Because she was a 37-year old woman living in an expensive city who wasn't sure she could support herself anymore.

Because she was, at heart, a loner, and often didn't mind the two solitudes of their marriage—Neil doing his own thing, she doing hers.

Because there were times, when Neil came home after a day at the races, sweltering under his leathers, unloading his bikes with arms that were more muscular and tawny than any of the other doughy, dutiful neighbourhood husbands, that she felt a surge of elemental pride that he was all man.

Because she couldn't stop him.

Her son, of course, would grow up to be a different kind of man. It was just the two of them, again, savouring another long fall afternoon in the neighbourhood park. Enclosed by oaks and maples and brilliant yellow elms, they sat on their favourite bench, reading a book they had just borrowed from the library. Pop-ups of classical buildings. Way too advanced for his seven years, but he already knew that he wanted to be an architect. With a soaring heart, she explained about domes and arches, Daniel taking in each word like a treat. Blocks away, traffic blared on busier streets. But their sanctum was soundproof, as if each gilded leaf were a deflecting shield.

* * *

"You're trying to turn him against me," Neil said—although he was impressed that Daniel could draw a Doric column and got raves from his teachers at school.

"I am not. Why can't you just accept the fact that he has different interests than you?"

"It's your fault he didn't like the race track."

"No, it's not my fault, Neil. Some people just don't like the noise. I don't like it."

They both backed off from the loaded topic of Daniel's first trip to the racetrack when he was four. Ears clutched to ward off the roar of 28 motorcycles leaving the start line, his crying as the screeching sliced in. Neil had ridden exceptionally well, coming in second place, his best finish in years. Daniel, his face buried in Carol's quilted jacket the entire time, hadn't seen any of it.

"I just get this feeling that you want him all to yourself sometimes."

"I don't want him all to myself. I want you to spend more time with him. I want you for once to spend a whole weekend with him without running off to do something connected with those stupid bikes. How hard can that be?"

* * *

Carol wanted Neil at home, yet couldn't stand him being at home. At least not during February, that long, drawn-out month where the racing dates were marked in his calendar, but the tracks were locked in ice. Everything was ready for race season—the valves ground, leathers patched, race videos analyzed, garage floor swept so clean you could eat off it—but still another month to go before the tracks opened. For weeks, sub-zero weather had leeched the life out of everyone. But not Neil, who shot out of bed at five, even on weekends.

That Saturday he was taking Daniel to see the gladiator exhibit at the museum. Something she should be happy about, but she woke up feeling apprehensive. She found Neil in the kitchen, staked out in front of the open fridge, scowling at something in the side door compartment. Daniel was in the living room immersed in cartoons. Pouring herself a cup of coffee, she sat down at the table and murmured good morning. Neil peered more pointedly into the fridge, and pulled his lips down in niggling reproach.

"Are you looking for something?" she finally asked.

"No. I just couldn't help but notice that you have five kinds of Dijon mustard in here," he said primly, taking out a jar of coarse-grained to conspicuously study the price tag.

"So? People like having a choice of mustards."

"I only mention it because you're always going on about how extravagant I am with my bikes."

The familiar anger buckled up, but Carol didn't rise to the bait. It was his favourite tactic, trying to justify the outrageous cost of his racing against her household expenses, one he had been milking ever since she recently went over-budget when renovating the kitchen. All she had left was to finish the curtains, and she planned to buy the material that afternoon. She looked at an ice-cankered window that needed covering, and told herself that Neil's crankiness was due to his frustration at not being able to race; a compulsive need to win at *something*, if only a stupid argument.

"Neil. You can't compare a three dollar mustard to seven hundred dollars for a pair of carburetors."

"But three times five equals fifteen. It all starts to add up."

"It's too early in the morning for this. Could you give it a rest?"

"Oh, I'll give it a rest," he replied, setting the mustard back with a lofty look of perceived triumph. "But the next time you start nagging me about how much money I spend on racing, I'll remind you of your *five* Dijons."

As petty as they were, Neil's comments undermined her shopping. Browsing through the fabric aisles, she felt outdated and idle, like one of those 1950s housewives who moved at a deliberately leisurely pace, less from calm than from the panic that if they hurried, they would bang into empty time. Her mood worsened as she thought of the two of them together. Was she really too possessive, wanting her son only for herself? Or was it protectiveness? As she chose bleached muslin (her second choice at 20 percent off), a small, spiteful side of her hoped that Daniel had overheard Neil picking on her. She imagined Daniel unhappy in his father's company, sensing his boredom and lack of knowledge of the historical exhibits, wishing he could be with her instead.

She had expected them home around four, but when she was taking a roast chicken out of the oven at six, Daniel flew through the front door, his cheeks aflame.

"Mommy! Daddy's going to buy me a Honda XR50!"

Studiously avoiding her eyes, Neil took off his boots in the hallway.

"What do you mean? I thought you were going to the museum."

"Oh, we saw the Roman exhibit," Neil said evenly, face still averted. "But after that we dropped by Ontario Honda."

"Daddy says that racing bikes is like racing chariots!"

The thought of her son straddling a motorcycle set Carol's mind reeling. Pulling down the fury in her voice, she said: "Daniel. You told me before. You never wanted to ride."

He gave her an apologetic shrug. But his face had a new caginess to it, a bright complicity in his saucer eyes.

"He can make up his own mind," Neil said gravely, intimating an exalted level of male bonding she couldn't possibly begin to understand.

"He's too young to make up his own mind! Is that what you've been doing all afternoon? Manipulating him into doing something he's terrified of?"

"He's only terrified of it, Carol, because that's what you've taught him."

"Neil, don't twist this ..."

"I don't need a motorcycle!" Daniel burst out, swerving in allegiance.

"Yes you do, Daniel, and it's none of your mom's fucking business!"

Good. He made a tactical error. Said the F-word. Daniel hated swearing, so the charmed web Neil had woven this afternoon was unravelling. By the flush on his neck, Carol saw that he had realized his mistake, and was struggling not to lose any more composure.

"I swear to God, Neil, if you've made a down payment on this bike ..."

"What are you going to do? Leave me?" he muttered, loud enough for only her to hear, before stalking off.

Daniel was now perched in the middle of the hall staircase, kneading the palm of his hand as if he intended to debone it. Carol pulled him toward her, and roughly kissed the top of his head.

"We're not mad at you, honey. But why don't you go to your room and read that book on buildings before supper? Mommy's just going to take a little walk."

To her sanctuary, the park, now a bed of blistered ice, encased in darkness. Hunched on her favourite bench, she considered divorcing Neil, denouncing him as an unfit father, going into the garage and smashing every one of those fucking bikes. Through the border of bare-black trees, she could see the brightly-lit windows of what could only be harmonious households, run by competent women. Beaming on her like interrogation lights, exposing all the weaknesses that let things get so out of hand.

When she got home, Neil was setting the table, his jaw clenched in sullen contriteness.

"I need to know. Did you put a down payment on that Honda?"

"No I didn't. Are you happy now?"

"In fact, I'm not. Is this what's going to happen whenever you take Daniel out? I won't be able to trust you with him?"

She expected anger, but his tone was weary, almost defeated. "How about when you're with him? How can I trust you not to make me out to be some speed obsessed"—he flinched at the word—"moron?"

"Well, what do you call racing around trying to kill yourself?"

"That's not what it's about. And that's what I really resent about you, Carol. You won't give me a chance to let Daniel understand my version of things."

* * *

At speeds over a hundred miles an hour, everything became slow motion. Neil said this was the result of having to be absorbed, for every single second, in every nuance of the ride: your position on the track, when to begin braking, when to step on the gas. For some riders, the intensity of concentration was metaphysical. As if the track had been immersed in a dense liquid, spaces opened, revealing entry points that had never existed before. Instead of the impenetrable cluster of riders ahead, you saw gaps that widened as you slipped through them. A sharp lean into a corner became a floating free fall until the bike tilted upright again. Within this suspended time, sound could be absent as well. And for a while, even the need to win dissolved, as the riders, bonded in the endless moment, completed lap after mesmerizing lap.

"But if everything is in slow motion, why are there still accidents?" Carol asked.

Another Saturday, this time ensconced in mutual well-being on the couch, starting a second bottle of white. Neil pondered the question, his features softening with the humbled calm of the enthralled. Hugging her more closely, he said: "Accidents are mainly a problem with the young guys who are a little too eager and are always trying to cut you off at corners. That's how I broke my collarbone two years ago. I got cut off by a 16-year-old."

"But Neil. You're 35. Your reflexes aren't the same as they once were."

"No, it's a fallacy that you get worse when you get older. In fact, the older and more experienced you are, the more likely you are to avoid a crash because you can see the pitfalls in advance."

"So you're saying you'll *never* be in an accident?" she asked, wanting to believe in the implausible reality of a safe competition, gentlemen riders in pursuit of a higher state of consciousness.

"What I'm saying is, with the experience I have now, it's not as strong a possibility."

* * *

In the racing videos, the accidents always looked cartoonish, cars spinning into the air, splay-legged bodies spilling out. Neil's accident was the most antic of all, with him flying over the handlebars as if he had just been shot out of a cannon.

And then landing on this hospital bed, face bruised, and with a brain that, according to the neurosurgery team, had been severely shaken and was swelling against the confines of his skull. A skull that was not smooth on the inside as she had always assumed, but jutting with bony protrusions around the eye and nose sockets, which caused fibre tearing. *Fibre tearing!* In her terror, all Carol could think about were the kitchen curtains she was sewing, how the threads got tangled in the needle plate.

Was this the third, fourth, or fifth day she had been

sitting at his bedside? As she flipped through a magazine, his eyes fluttered open.

"Neil. Do you know where you are?"

His irises were murky ponds, surrounded by a moat of chartreuse-coloured bruises. He looked at the wall, the wacky get-well card from Bob, and the stroke patient lying in the bed next to him.

"A convent," he said, his eyes falling shut again.

Carol gently tugged his arm. The nurses said that in the first days of recovery, it was important that he didn't sleep too much; he'd be at risk of falling into a coma.

"Neil. Please wake up, honey."

When they opened this time, his eyes were hostile and suspicious, probing her face with hard, narrowed blinks.

"Neil. Do you know who I am?" she asked, flinching.

"The devil," he replied, slipping into unconsciousness again.

* * *

There was a fear, a queasy knowledge growing that she may have caused the accident. The night she went into the garage and did—what? Broke something? Or just scraped it? Sometimes, just before she was about to drop off into a deep, exhausted sleep, a fragment of memory would pop up like a deranged jack in the box. Heart pounding, she would shove it back down again.

Besides which, there was no time to think. She had to arrange hospital visits, cancel photography bookings, fill out insurance forms, phone her old contacts in real estate because it seemed very likely that she would have to return to work again. Endless practical considerations that riveted the mind on something other than fear. She was on her way out the door in the second week of Neil's hospitalization when the phone rang. Trevor Peters, a client of Neil's, sounding harassed as he inquired about a photo for the Burger Barn Double Cheese Event.

"Neil is still in intensive care, Trevor …"

"Yes, I realize that, and I'm sorry to be bothering you. But he was supposed to have the finished file ready for my printer Friday, and no one at his studio seems to know which one it is."

"I'm not sure how I can help …"

"When will he be out of the hospital?" Trevor cut in.

"The doctors can't say," Carol replied helplessly, for this was their answer to everything: we can't say, we can't say, we can't say.

"Well, when you see Neil, could you please ask him if he remembers where he put the Burger Barn file?"

He can't even remember that he's a photographer, she wanted to snap. Yet she couldn't let Neil's clients know the full extent of his injury, make assumptions about his capabilities when—or if—he was ever able to return to work. Another chute of terror opened. What if Neil didn't regain his intellectual faculties? Became a drooling idiot, incapable of doing anything but the simplest tasks? "*Moron*," she could hear him saying accusingly. "You wanted to make me look like a moron in front of my son."

"I'll ask him about it," she said, feeling as though she would pass out from guilt.

Trevor's voice rose in reedy impatience. "Thank you. And could you please remind him that this coupon is *important*."

* * *

When visiting hours were over, the intensive care ward became strangely comforting, the stricken whispers and reassurances of consolers replaced by the steady hum of doctors and nurses maintaining an illusion of control. At least that's how Carol felt this night, reluctant to leave the false calm of Neil's beside for the uncertainties of the outside world. Exhausted by a rash of visitors he no longer recognized, Neil had fallen into a deep sleep. Carol compulsively tidied up around him, while Daniel examined the bed fixtures, a fascination with hospital gadgetry temporarily allaying fears about his father.

"Mommy. Can I press the button to raise daddy's bed?" he asked.

"Yes, honey. But don't jerk it, OK? You don't want to hurt daddy."

Neil's eyes popped open and stared at her in pure bewilderment.

"Carol. Why does my head hurt?"

He remembered her name! Hope coursed through her, but she kept her voice even, as if too much emotion would tip over the newly constructed memory circuits.

"You crashed your motorcycle, Neil. You're in the hospital with a head injury."

"I crashed my bike?"

"At Shannonville. This happened two weeks ago."

"The Ducati? I crashed my Ducati?"

"You've been in the hospital all this time, honey."

Daniel, still too riveted by the controls to appreciate a neurological breakthrough, touched Neil on the arm. "Daddy. Can I raise the bed higher?"

"Just a little bit, Daniel," Neil replied, completely flummoxed. He rubbed his forehead, as if that would help clear things up. "Have I really been in the hospital for two weeks?"

"You were in a very serious accident, Neil. You could have died."

"What about my work?"

"It's OK, Neil. It's been taken care of."

Understanding rolled in, then horror, his eyes becoming enlarged and sombre against his yellowing bruise.

"You must be very angry with me," he said simply.

* * *

The medical literature on head injuries cautioned about too much optimism in the beginning. Microscopic nerve damage couldn't always be detected, but could cause long-term problems with thinking, motor skills, and emotional control. Often these problems didn't turn up until the person returned to the demands of the working day and found himself confused and unable to concentrate—all of which could lead to depression or abusive behaviour.

Sobered by these statistics, Carol was often struck with gratitude so profound it pinned her to the spot in prayer. According to their neurosurgeon, it was remarkable that Neil could return to work only six months after his injury, no repercussions except for decreased stamina and mental fatigue in the evenings. Then there was his new emotional maturity, the way he quietly advertised his beloved bikes in the classifieds, and sold them one by one.

Almost as if you had planned it that way, people joked with her.

* * *

Carol braced herself for another account of the accident. A blow-by-blow rendition she had heard countless times, and which, until recently, she would immediately tune out. Darkness was coming in, dissolving the last pink smudges of sunset over the lake. Pouring Neil another cup of coffee, she watched Bob light a cigarette, then squint dramatically out at the water. He had seen everything from the front row bleachers, and relished this vantage point in what had become, in Neil's racing circle, a myth-making event.

"You were heading into the corner, and then you were flying over the handlebars," he recounted, shooting his arm up in the air for emphasis as he always did.

Neil shook his head and frowned. "That's what I don't understand. I've always been cautious on the first corner. Probably too cautious, which is why I never get a good lead. I know I didn't accelerate too hard."

"And you didn't graze anyone. Didn't graze a soul."

"Yet somehow my front wheel came out from under me ..."

"Then bam! One minute you were on the track, the next minute you were ten feet up into the air!"

"I wonder if there was a problem with my bike," Neil said, just as she knew he would. Excusing herself, she got up from the table and headed for the dock where the boys were clearing up the rubbery remains of water balloons.

* * *

That day, that hot, muggy August day just over a year ago, she was on the patio, registering for a course in classical art.

Daniel approached her clutching a piece of paper. A drawing, she thought, but the nervous way he handed it to her told her otherwise. Marching down the page, large carefully printed letters explained why he wanted to learn how to ride: To learn a new skill. To excel. To have a new hobby. "Daddy said you would be mad if I told you I wanted a motorcycle," he blurted out when he saw her stricken look. "So he had me write out the reasons and give them to you."

She found Neil in the garage, shining the bike he was going to ride in next Saturday's race, a preening red and green Ducati. It rose like a monument on its stand in front of the other six motorcycles that were lined up against the wall. On his worktable lay a bright plastic decal, the number 22 that would go onto the front fender of the Ducati. Giving her an unreadable look, he picked up a utility knife and began cutting out the number.

"I guess you're going to buy Daniel a bike now."

"He seems to want it. He came to me asking. I didn't come to him."

She knew this was probably true. Ever since he had turned eight in June, Daniel's passions had evolved from stationary to moving constructions. It was bound to happen, wanting to feel the levers that powered vehicles, to experience their force.

Her hands clenched into impotent little fists, the smells of engine oil and cleaning solvent spiking her sinuses. Even in the summer light, the garage exterior looked dark and moist, like the belly of a mythic whale, partially digested bike parts winking in its depths.

"If you buy Daniel a motorcycle, I'll leave you," she said, stunned by how lamely it came out, this long-rehearsed threat.

Neil paused for an instant, then bore down harder on

the knife. She watched the blade sink through the plastic onto the worktable, making a resistant, tugging sound as it sliced through the wood.

"Are you going to buy Daniel the bike?"

"I'm going to listen to what he wants for a change," he replied without looking up.

A woman, it must have been her, was in the garage later that night. Immobilized in a state between blinding rage and mortification, not quite sure of what she intended to do with the utility knife she was gripping in one hand. The garage was pitch-black, incubated in diesel smells. Only by the ghostly gleams of handlebars and chrome could she make out where the bikes were. She could feel them though. Huddled against the wall in their inviolable camaraderie like some smirking street gang. Sneering at her. At her ineptness, the way she just stood there, grasping at surfaces, terrified of knocking something over and waking Neil. The thought of how ridiculous she must look reasserted itself, and she panicked, wanting to leave. But no ... something. She had to hurt something. The blade jabbed a hard rubbery darkness that felt like a tire, and jerked back. Then the knife was back on the workbench, and she was hurrying back to the house.

That Saturday Neil had the accident. Coincidence she would tell herself, hurtling into another task to keep the unthinkable at bay.

* * *

Across the lake, other cottages twinkled in the dark like a string of fairy lights. Check the bunkie to see if the boys are sleeping, Carol thought, but she remained at the picnic table with Neil and Bob, nursing a cold cup of coffee. The quiet thickened as conversation petered out, mostly in deference to Neil, who, as on most evenings, was now having problems putting a sentence together. His face looked visibly strained as if a drawstring were cinched around his forehead, keeping the contents from spilling out. But there was none of his old irritability, and he grinned with sheepish resignation every time he stumbled over a word, believing he had brought it on himself.

He got up from the table. "Well, I'm off to bed now. Can't do late nights anymore."

She wanted to follow him. Hold him tightly; cradle his head the way she would a baby's, keep him safe and sound all night. Bob lit a cigarette, the last in his pack. A sharp queasiness hit, as if she wanted to throw up not only the contents of her stomach, but her bones and sinews too. Striving for a jocular tone, she said: "Bob. I was thinking about what you said about the crash earlier on."

"What about it?"

"Well, it just seems so strange ... the way it happened."

Bob's hand shot up. "One minute on the track. The next, ten feet in the air!"

"Could there have been a problem with one of the tires beforehand? Could it have been punctured?"

"Punctured?"

"Like by a nail," she added quickly. "If that had happened, could it have caused the crash?"

Bob regarded her more closely. "It could have."

She nodded and turned her face to the lake. Stupid, stupid, for her to have asked, to have aroused suspicion!

Even so, she couldn't be sure what tire she jabbed. There were at least five bikes in the garage that night, and she couldn't make out a thing. How could she be sure it was the Ducati tire?

When it came out again, her voice skittered out of her throat like something slingshot into the night sky. "Wouldn't Neil have taken a few practice laps first? If there was a puncture, wouldn't he have discovered it then?"

"Not necessarily. It all depends on where the puncture was and how deep it went."

Carol stayed focused on the lake, grateful when she spotted a piece of water balloon, for it gave her an excuse to get out of the range of what she was convinced was Bob's scrutiny. Conscious of trying to look like a normal mother cleaning up after a normal day at the cottage, she bent down to pick up a rubber bit.

And a memory of that night rushed in again. This time better lit. She saw her eyes adjusting to the darkness, dimly able to make out details. A leather seat. A front fender. The number 22 on the Ducati. The image hovered at the end of a long tunnel in her mind, as if awaiting permission to attach itself to another image of herself about to step toward the fender. Quickly she blinked it away.

"I'm just glad he got better," she said, pretending to scour the ground for more pieces.

"Oh, that was some knock on the head!" Bob said with a laugh.

Lord of the Manor

It was an accident that Adam discovered the house was for sale. He had been designing a real estate brochure, a pleasantly mindless task that involved arranging tiny photos of properties with little blocks of type below them. His office, just off the master bedroom, was a converted gentleman's study. Even his computer looked antique in the soft June sunlight that was burnishing the room. He was so snugly ensconced in his well being that he almost didn't recognize his home when it appeared on the screen. *"Circa 1900 Stone Manor House. Panoramic View of Niagara Escarpment. $785,000."* For a long while, he could only stare at the photo, checking every cherished architectural detail to make sure there was no mistake. Then he copied the page and emailed it to his landlord, signing it simply with a large question mark.

"Oh, it's just speculation to see what the house is worth," his wife Eleanor insisted later that evening as they cleared up the supper dishes.

"Then there's also the matter that we still have three years left on our lease," Adam said, surprised that the landlord, whom he considered a friend, had not gotten back to them.

They both spoke casually so as not to attract the attention of their son James who was in the adjoining living room hunched over an intricate Lego ship he had been building for hours. At six years old, he possessed an ability for sustained concentration that both parents lacked; the result, Adam felt, of having spent the last two years in a tranquil country environment. In fact, when Adam thought about what he loved about the place, its history, natural beauty, and the genteel farming community, it was all in relation to how it would shape his son's character. Their big project this summer was to build a fort in the nearby woods and, in his spare time, Adam had been collecting lumber in his shed.

"It has never felt as though we were *renting* this house," Eleanor said, placing a creamer into the pantry.

Adam nodded, flinching at the word "rent." How intrusive it sounded, with its other meaning, to rip, tear asunder, ruin. And to find out through a brochure he was designing! He thought of the photo, how magnificent the house looked perched on the hill. Could he Photoshop it to make it look less appealing? Darken it? Make it grainy? No, it was best to wait until he spoke to the landlord before doing anything hasty.

"Besides which," Eleanor said, "it's priced way too high. Who has that kind of money these days?"

"Not us," Adam sighed, getting up to join his son in the living room. "It will certainly never be us."

But then, the accumulation of wealth had never been Adam's goal. He had grown up in a small meatpacking town where sons followed fathers into the plant like cattle. Adam's fear of being locked into one thing had led to a knack of picking up many things easily: at 39, he could boast of having had a dozen careers, including social worker, photographer's assistant, radio announcer, set decorator and, most recently, graphic designer. He had been working as a carpenter on a historical movie when he met Eleanor, a prop girl. At the end of filming, they were living together in an apartment furnished with choice antiques they had discreetly lifted from the set and charged to the movie's budget.

And now they had leading roles in their own historical setting! Adam never tired of telling how they had arrived at the point of charmed stability. He had been fired from an advertising agency in Toronto, a pressure magnified by the fact that he was now supporting Eleanor, whom he had married, and James, who was four years old. Hoping to get some freelance work, he had driven out to the Grey County area to meet a prospective client who sold agricultural products. It had been a beautiful day, clouds docked like cruise ships in the green hills. He passed gingerbread farmhouses, red barns, racing stables, apple orchards and, overlooking it all, the manor house, with—could it be?—a For Rent sign out front. When he phoned the landlord and discovered that it rented for the same price as their Toronto apartment, he hadn't the slightest hesitation on what he was going to do next.

* * *

This night, though, there was. In just two days, prospective buyers would be ogling the view, which this evening dazzled; the hills haloed in amber light, coins of gold sunset glinting through the trees. Eleanor stood at the

French doors that opened out onto the terrace, and frowned at Adam seated at the dining room table.

"We have to make them think that this is one of those old, mouldering houses that needs a lot of work," she said.

"It does need a lot of work! It needs more insulation around the windows and a windbreak for that west wall, which I've already devoted considerable time and effort to!"

He tried not to think about the landlord, a stockbroker his age who owned three other investment properties. "Just testing the market to see what the house is worth," had been his overly hearty explanation to Adam's email. "Nothing serious!"

Then why go to the expense of putting an ad in a glossy brochure, Adam had been too afraid to ask. And our five-year lease? A mere trifle? Quickly, even sloppily, he had finished designing the brochure, sent it off to the client, then concentrated on planning James' tree fort. When he had almost forgotten about the ad, the realtor called to book a showing.

"If the house looked like it had major problems ... maybe something wrong with the septic system ... that's fairly common out here, "Eleanor said.

"We could throw shit on the walls," Adam shrugged facetiously.

"Or give it a bad smell."

"A bad smell would be nice."

Eleanor squinted at the driveway beyond the terrace. After a long pause, she casually said: "Dead groundhogs give off a bad smell. We could always put one by an air vent."

"Yes, we could do that," Adam said just as offhandedly.

"Well, we *could*."

In the waning light, her eyes resembled the dark slits of a cartoon villain. Looking away, Adam thought of James who was upstairs playing with his train set. Arrangements had been made so that he would be at a neighbour's farm when the prospective buyers arrived, so he wouldn't worry that something out of the ordinary was developing. After that, they would start laying the foundation for his fort in the woods.

"In fact, when I was pulling up the driveway today I noticed a dead groundhog on the side of the road," Eleanor said.

"How convenient."

"It'd be easy enough to do. You would just have to pick it up with a shovel and set it by the basement air vent."

Adam looked down at their dining room table, an original Hepplewhite with matching sideboard. It had been Eleanor's idea to cart them home in the movie van after the last day of filming; something that now seemed so totally out of character for him, he didn't like to think about it around his son. He put on an aloof expression to distance himself from her suggestion. But to his relief, she buried her face in her hands, and laughed. "I can't believe we're talking like this!"

* * *

The odour that emanated from the dead groundhog was surprisingly authentic—not a strong animal stench at all, but musty, sweetly decaying, redolent of ancient rot and mildewing wood. No room was free from its fine, cloying scent. In an ingenious touch, Eleanor had sprayed the house with a lilac air freshener to suggest they had to deal with the smell daily. When Adam announced that a car was pulling up into the driveway, she gave the kitchen one last vigorous spray, then set the floral can prominently on the kitchen counter.

Adam opened the door to an efficient-looking female realtor and a well-dressed couple of retirement age. The husband didn't appear to notice the smell at all. But both women did; an unmistakable flinching of the nostrils, puzzled frowns, quick, polite smiles. Eleanor put on a remarkable performance, showing off the study, the sunroom, the renovated servant's quarters. They stayed for half an hour, the husband examining the structure of the walls, the wife the wainscotting. When the realtor asked if they wanted to see the basement, they declined. "Oh, it's really not that good for storage anyway," Eleanor cooed in her plushest tones. "With all the space here, we *rarely* use it."

And then the intruders were gone, the walls seeming to quiver as if they too had been holding something in. For a week, Adam went through the motions of his everyday life, waiting for the landlord to call. What if the realtor had alerted him to the odour? He had a plausible excuse; some animal had died nearby and the smell had lingered in the warm weather. But his only calls were work-related. Could it really be that easy?

Two weeks later, the realtor phoned again. A couple from West Virginia this time. Horse people up here for the races. People who owned *homes*. Could they come around to look next Wednesday?

* * *

Adam adjusted the rifle on his back and stepped out of his car into a cornfield. After weeks of glorious sun, it was abruptly fall-like, the sky colourless, a chill in the air. Road-side plants looked both bristling and resigned at the un-seasonable lack of light. And in the trenches, roads, and fields he had been scouring all morning, not one dead groundhog was to be found.

He pressed on past fields of cornstalks, their leaves curled under like fists, as if enraged at their dependence on unpredictable weather conditions.

He had always assumed that the entire Grey County area was picturesque, but it wasn't. Here, only a few kilo-metres from where they lived, there was a drab flatness to the land that made it look like the outskirts of any indus-trial town. Just like the one he had grown up in. He had barely noticed the houses before, except as bucolic back-ground, but driving past them while searching for ground-hogs, he realized he was appraising them as potential places to rent. Even without glancing into the windows, he knew what they were about. Linoleum floors. Stained bathtubs. Orange shag carpets. *Smells.* The premature fall weather seemed part of a conspiracy to keep everything in its place, to not let anything grow beyond a pre-determined size. Stopping, Adam scanned a field for the familiar dark, rounded shape, not quite believing he would actually shoot a groundhog if he found a live one.

"Daddy. Is the house going to be sold?" James had asked Adam earlier that morning when after an hour of fruit-lessly searching the grounds of the manor house, he had gone to the shed to get his rifle.

"What makes you think that?" he had replied, avoiding

his son's eyes. There was too much probing in them, analysis; eyes that would patiently examine even the empty spaces in a Lego construction to better understand how it all fit together.

"I don't know."

"Did you see a 'For Sale' sign in front of it?"

"No."

"Then it's not going to be sold."

The lie knotted in his chest. What if Adam let him down? What if his much-anticipated fort was never built? What if his son started judging him the way he judged his own father?

Adam rarely thought about his parents, but the landscape was unearthing buried realizations—such as the fact that he had virtually ignored his father for the past 20 years, rarely visiting him except for the odd Christmas. "A man who made baloney for a living," was how he described him. A man who could watch hair, hoofs, and snouts churn into a vat of pink sludge, then eat a Spam sandwich for lunch. Over the years, Adam had come to view his father as a cardboard figure from which he could project his infinite capacity for reinventing himself. Yet here he was, intending to slaughter an animal.

He had always prided himself on being a genial guy, even in adversity. Now a surprising bitterness rose, feeling like the vein of some hard, yet worthless metal; a shaft aimed for his heart. All his life he had resisted being stuck in a single identity. Was this the culmination, to be stripped of the one that mattered most to him? His plans for James' security built on shifting sand?

Go home, he told himself. Not being able to find a groundhog was an omen, a sign to let things take their course.

But at the same time he felt enraged that something so simple was being denied him, a premonition of future failure.

The cornstalks shuddered in a sudden gust of wind. Go home, he told himself more firmly. And still scouring the fields, he headed for his car.

* * *

James followed Adam down the front hall, past the kitchen, toward the basement. "But I want to know why you did it!" he kept demanding.

Adam stood at the basement door, not quite able to place his hand on the knob. How portentous it looked, as if it belonged to the entrance of some secret chamber! And was that really his voice, so weak and hovering, ordering his son back to his room? James stood his ground, appraising Adam, his cheeks blotchy with panic and confusion. When he reluctantly turned back down the hall, Adam stepped into the basement, quickly shutting the door behind him.

Here the smell was electric, his nostrils charged. Thanks to last night's humidity, the stench now penetrated every room in the house like some fine internal wiring. Adam's throat clamped reflexively against the stink. But he forced himself to take deep breaths, needing to acknowledge the full measure of his mistake.

The groundhog he had spotted yesterday while driving home now lay in a dark stain by the air vent. From the back, it appeared to be dozing. But drawing closer, Adam saw the bullet holes, spilt guts, and the hind foot twisted up at a grotesque right angle.

He would never forgive himself for breaking the groundhog's foot. The inept first shot that had wrenched it backward, sending the animal scuttling away on exposed bone. Adam had chased it, blasting and blasting until it had finally fallen beside a clump of earth. He knew the bloody carcass should have remained where it was. But a mix of emotions, anger at his ineptitude, a perverse fatalism, and a stubborn refusal to let the animal's death be in vain had all intervened, and picking it up by the scruff of the neck, he had carried it back to his car.

Above him, he could hear Eleanor dragging their big floor fan into the living room to try to disperse the odour. She had already sprayed the house with air freshener, desperately this time, the lilac scent crackling against the underlying putrid mass like makeup on a crone's face. Their only hope was to get the appointment moved to another day. Every two minutes she would rush back to the phone to contact the realtor who still wasn't answering her cell.

"You don't put a festering, bleeding groundhog by an air vent all night!" she had railed at Adam earlier that morning, right in front of James.

"It wasn't my idea to do it in the first place," he had retorted almost primly.

"But I didn't tell you to do it a second time! We could get evicted for this!"

"What's eviction?" James asked, blinking furiously, as if it would help him process everything faster.

"It's when your landlord kicks you out of your house!" Eleanor had cried, shooting an accusing look at Adam.

"Are we going to get kicked out of our house, Daddy?"

"No, we're not, James. Now could you please not go near the basement?"

He picked up the shovel that lay against the wall. Gently, as if the animal could still feel pain, he slipped the tip under its hindquarters. However, the movement only succeeding in dislodging a fetid gush of slime that seeped into the cracks on the cement floor. Positioning the tip more securely under the carcass, he attempted another lift. Then, suddenly, he was hit by a memory.

He saw himself at six years old, visiting his father at the slaughterhouse. Almost passing out from the stench. His father, calmly mopping up innards, explained that what Adam smelled was mostly urine. Cows pissing themselves in panic before they died, he had chuckled, expecting Adam to laugh too. It had been a defining moment of his childhood, and he had vowed never to be like his father. He could remember willing the separation between them, making the psychological pulling away so fervent that it almost had a sound to it like masking tape being ripped from a wall.

Now he became aware of his own son watching him. Peering through a crack in the basement door, his alarm overridden by his natural curiosity about the way things worked, about what was going on.

"Daddy. Why did you put a dead groundhog in the basement?" James asked with a calculated sombreness designed to engage Adam in one of their talks.

Adam looked away. James would figure it out for himself when the realtor arrived, which would likely be any moment now. He aimed foolishly for a reassuring, fatherly tone, knowing it would never be fully trusted again.

"James. Could you please go to your room? Could you please just go?"

"But I want to know *why!*" James cried, rising up in a huff. And Adam stood, breathing in guts, thinking he could almost hear it again—the familiar tearing sound of a young boy distancing himself from what he never wanted to be.

Dissolution

~~~~~

Nine a.m., scorching sun already bleaching out the few clouds trying to assert themselves on a hazy sky. Janet pumped the gas and turned down another tony Rosedale street, past homes tucked in tree banks that were voluminous in the humidity, long caverns of shade in their swollen depths. She was grateful for her early morning appointment, its promise of structure for the rest of the day. Steve stood waiting for her in his driveway; a compact, muscular man wearing black bathing trunks, arms folded across his tanned chest and radiating such bedrock well-being that it looked as though *he* should be giving this yoga class.

"Sounds like your car's getting ready to die there," he said, as she parked with a splutter behind his gray BMW.

"Hey, why not? Everything else in my life has."

He stepped back. "Shit Janet. I'm sorry."

"No, *I'm* sorry. You didn't mean it that way," she said quickly. It was selfish to make others feel bad for not being attuned to the minute permutations of grief, which she was still going through a year and a half after Daniel's death. "How is your back? Is it feeling better?"

"Almost ready to do the Kama Sutra again!"

"That's gooood," she said, although that it wasn't true. Steve was a long time, yet sporadic, client, calling only when his back acted up. Lingering pain meant repeat business for her.

Sweat beaded between her small breasts and trickled down into the band of the black sports bra she wore with matching biking shorts. Beyond the driveway lay water, the glittering strip of turquoise pool.

Steve glanced at his watch, then at her. "Ready to roll?"

She started. Had she just spaced out staring at the water? Floated out of time again?

"Um, oh yeah. You bet! Let's get going!"

An hour later, she was in the pool, having convinced Steve that the water would help limber up his muscles in the final poses. The session over, he was on the patio, yammering into his cell about some new software gizmo he was marketing that would change the way people worked and lived. Floating on her back, careful not to get her hair too wet, she watched him, grateful that his talking gave her more time in the water. From behind, he looked as if he could be in his late twenties rather than his late forties, like her. He had never settled down after his second divorce, something she had not paid much attention to before, but which now seemed laden with incoherent possibility. When they were doing the final poses, she had lightly—as she did with all clients—touched the sides of his waist to keep his spine properly aligned. In the water, her fingers looked pickled and white, separate from her body, his bathing trunks, similarly distorted, floating up to meet them. For a half moment, she wondered, what if her hands were to slip *down there*? But for what? Sex? More money tacked onto the measly forty dollars she'd receive for this session? An invitation to hang out in the pool for the rest of the afternoon? As if picking up on the deliberately vague intentions of her southbound poised fingers, Steve tensed. Like startled fish, her hands darted to his ribcage to guide him into a counter-stretch, gently now, *gently*; he had to honour the pain in his back.

He was off the phone now, a preoccupied look on his face as he grabbed a fresh towel from the back of a deck chair. "Hey, don't get too comfortable in there, kiddo. I've got to get to a meeting pronto."

"Me too," she said, although the only business she had this afternoon was placing her flyers in health food stores across the city. She had a sudden urge to urinate in the water, defile it, ruin something beautiful, just as Daniel had been ruined. Instead, she clambered out and accepted the towel Steve held out for her, vigorously rubbing her sports bra and shorts, hoping the Spandex would dry quickly.

The pool sparkled in its emptiness, large, neon white squiggles, like an abstract painting continually reconfiguring into new shapes. A seal, a starburst, and now what looked like the outline of a body.

"It's so peaceful here," she said.

"Yeah. And most of the people who live here go to their cottages for the summer, so this neighbourhood is as quiet as a tomb ... sorry."

"Hey, that's OK."

He handed her two crisp twenties from his wallet. "Shall we set up an appointment for another session?" she asked.

It came out sounding desperate, as if she was asking him for a date. A thin pad of pool water had collected in the crotch of her shorts, but she felt self-conscious about towelling between her legs again, and concentrated on drying her shins.

"I'm out of town for the next couple of days. I'll call you."

* * *

Outside the leafy dome of Rosedale, the air was instantly foul, granular with pollution. The drive to Noah's Health Food Store in the Annex scoured the last traces of clean chlorine scent off her skin. Parking, she grabbed some flyers from the back seat. The last time she'd been here was to find a protein drink, which was all Daniel's body could absorb in its final stages of pancreatic cancer, one of the most virulent ones, with a prognosis of eight weeks by the time he was diagnosed. But even that had been too optimistic; he had only lasted five.

The store was empty save for a new sales clerk she didn't know, a young woman standing behind the cash register. She barely glanced at Janet. Above the juice bar, hung the bulletin board, blossoming with glossy brochures. Goddess Yoga. Flow Yoga. Power Yoga. All more professional looking than hers, and not one space left.

She sunk down into a chair, immobilized by the thought that every bulletin board in every health store in the city might be like this. *What do I do* now *Daniel?* She usually felt—or tried to feel—that he was watching out for her, but was keenly aware of his absence today. That business in the pool, for example. Nothing had happened. Nothing was going to happen ... but still. As if to reproach her, the crotch of her shorts remained damp, forming a lewd looking triangle of darker black.

And now she was aware that the young clerk *was* looking at her, with the averted nervous glance of strangers, people who didn't know her story, sensing that something was off about her, but not sure what it could be. She crossed her legs, the familiar shakiness settling in. It had been a mistake to cremate Daniel, dispersing his ashes into the air, precious particles of him now lodged in other people's lungs. She should have kept his ashes in a vial around her neck that she could snort like coke when she needed the comfort of his common sense inside her.

Folding 30 of her flyers, these cheap photocopies that had no place here, had taken an entire day. No one had warned her about the ungainliness of grief, how it made one clumsy, how she, who could hold a handstand for 15 minutes, was sometimes rendered unwieldy as a sack of potatoes. She longed to go home and sleep, but somehow stayed in the chair. Any moment now, the young woman was going to clear her throat, and ask her if she could help her with something.

Clutching her flyers, she hauled herself up, releasing, she was certain, a pungent cloud of drying Spandex and vaginal moisture. *Sorry, sorry, sorry,* she found herself whispering to no one in particular, the way she often did these days, imagining the girl furiously wiping off the chair after she left.

* * *

A purification of sorts had been Janet's goal when she met Daniel at a yoga ashram in India in the early 80s. She had just left her boyfriend—three years of travelling together that had ended abruptly in a Bangkok hotel room. Daniel barely registered with her at first. She was dedicated to doing the poses with the total absorption the yogi asked of them, maintaining a rhythm that promised freedom from the impulses of the body. Yoga made her clear-headed: an unfamiliar sensation of capability she often dulled by smoking weed. After class, Daniel would sit in the courtyard, slightly aloof from the rest of the group, his monkish, shaved head bent over a tiny book on Mandarin. Remote, but not oblivious to her, a taut, toned redhead travelling solo—a rarity for women in those days. When he asked her if she had any plans after the Ashram, she shrugged; she could stay here forever riding the currents of her ever-refined breath, although she was running out of money. He had a job teaching English in a town a few miles away—would she like to come along? Two years later, when he was offered a job teaching ESL classes in Toronto, she came along too.

* * *

Her car was parked at the end of the block, where a group of kids were slumped along the wall of a bank building. Homeless, by the looks of it. One of the girls had long black hair swept up into a ponytail, and a high forehead that Janet could see, even from half a block away, swelled slightly in profile, catching the light. Oh god, not here. Please, not *her*! After all this time, Janet couldn't run into Angela right now, wet crotch, god knows what expression on her face. She considered crossing the street, but there were too many cars all of a sudden, every one of them speeding. The sun, a burning sheet of metal, propelled her down the sidewalk toward the kids. A few feet away from the girl, she noted with relief the spotty skin and thin lips—not Angela after all. Back in her car, she collapsed, rocking back and forth, trying to catch her breath.

* * *

It was Daniel's idea for her to apply for the yoga teacher position at The Home, a halfway house for homeless teenage girls, which had recently received almost a million dollars in government funding. Who better qualified than Janet, who had lived on the streets when she left home at 17? Who had put in countless volunteer hours on distress lines, soup kitchens, native drop-in and rape crisis centres? Who still dreamed of getting a degree in counselling as a mature student? Janet, however, had never held a full-time job, a deficiency that became evident when she tried to put together a resume. With Daniel's help, the dribs and drabs of her experience, the holes in her education, her life, somehow added up to a plausible whole. She was called for an interview.

The Home was located in a renovated warehouse on King Street West. The program director, a Mr. Ron Richardson, roughly her age, conducted the interview in his second-floor office. A player, Janet thought, taking in his tallness, his preppie good looks, his carefully pressed denim shirt worn with a red schoolboy tie and, of course, the reason he was interviewing her, and not the other way round, the requisite Master's degree in social work prominently displayed on the wall behind his desk. Never once spending a day on the poverty line, but rich in the political acumen that people like her lacked to market themselves to the powers that bestowed big money.

Evidently much of the funding had gone into creating a bulwark of paper—policy manuals, conduct manuals, staff manuals—towers of them, neatly stacked on the credenza behind his desk.

After a brief sales talk about The Home's goal of reintegration, Ron drew her resume from a folder thick with other applications. He had the kind of mouth she disliked in a man, lips turned down in a look of cultivated withholding. "I see you've done a fair amount of work with the elderly," he said after a lengthy pause.

"Yes, and I still do work for the Lung Association. With rehab patients."

"I worked as a physical therapist at an old folks home when I was in college."

"Yes, and I love working with the elderly because ..." She stopped. She almost said, 'because I know they need me.' " Because you know, it's so rewarding."

"And what inspired you to apply to The Home, Janet?" he asked with exaggerated casualness.

This was the standard question for anyone working in youth organizations, designed to ferret out pervs. Janet had dealt with it dozens of times. Still she stumbled on her answer. "Well, I've always been attracted to youth ... I mean, working with youth. I was a street kid for a while when I was younger, so I think I can relate to these girls."

Ron frowned, and clasped his hands over her resume. "In our program, we're trying very hard not to use labels such as 'street kids.' We want our clients to see themselves as contributing members of society."

Like I'm too stupid to figure that out, she wanted to snap. But through Daniel, she was still learning not to take such things so personally. Her eyes went to a particularly officious looking tower of royal blue manuals. *Rules of Conduct for Part-Time Staff and Volunteers.*

"No, of course. I understand and respect that."

"We feel that offering structured activities is very important for our clients—especially on the weekend. That's why we've expanded our program to include a Saturday morning class."

She nodded, bristling again at the notion of yoga being lumped into the "activities" category, along with crafts or volleyball. She believed (but had learned better than to say) that teaching yoga was a grave responsibility because certain poses could release blocked memories. Ten years ago, when she had returned to school to try for a psych degree, she had written a paper on Wilhelm Reich, the pioneering psychiatrist of the 1930s who believed that repressed, traumatic emotions are held or "armoured" in the body, and that touch, or certain movements, could break down that armour. "This is still speculation, naive and dangerous at that," her professor had written, giving her a C– that prompted her to drop out of university altogether.

Ron suddenly broke into a small grin. "And I see you've been checked," he said.

"Checked?"

"Police clearance. It's mandatory for anyone working at The Home as it is with any youth organization."

"Oh yeah. I'm definitely cool with the police. Paid up all my parking tickets."

She expected a chortle, but his face closed into studied implacability, as he slipped her resume back into her folder.

"We're still narrowing our candidates, but we will call you and let you know our decision. Thank you again for coming down, Janet."

* * *

Fifteen girls showed up for The Home's first Saturday morning yoga class, held in a small gym three doors down from Ron's office. Sprites, Janet thought as they trooped in, most of them tiny, pocket-sized girls, used to curling up in doorways, car seats, other people's couches, taking up as little space as possible. With bouncy, near-identical names like Gaela, Kalea, and Delea. Considering she'd taught hundreds of classes, Janet was unexpectedly nervous. Watching them line up their mats, she promptly forgot everyone's name except for Sunshine, a short, stocky girl in the first row.

The most unfortunately named girl in the world, she'd tell Daniel later. Sunshine was almost aggressively dour; her stomach already sinking into a middle-aged paunch, her lank hair, narrowed eyes, even her baggy sweatpants and T-shirt, all blending into a puddle-brown shade that looked as if it had never absorbed a ray of light.

Janet turned on her music, soft Tibetan flute tones, and cleared her throat.

"Before we begin our postures, does anyone have any injuries or conditions I should know about?"

Sunshine's hand instantly shot up—allergies to fragrances, a sore left elbow from a bicycle accident, a bad back.

"Thank you, Sunshine. I'll watch for that. Anybody else? OK then, let's begin! Let's start by lying down in the ashana posture. Flat on our mats, arms at our sides, palms up."

She asked them to take ten deep breaths, paying attention to how the breath flowed down to the belly. From there, she had them gently roll up into a forward standing stretch that allowed her to observe misalignments in the body.

Sunshine's tailbone was already too high, straining her fragile lower back muscles, which were pulled down by the weight of her stomach. Padding over to her, Janet addressed the class.

"I'm going to do something called a 'touch-assist.' What this means is that I'll help you in a pose if I think you might strain or hurt yourself. If anyone is uncomfortable with being touched, please let me know."

The gym door had a small window, which made her slightly paranoid that she was being watched—especially as she had seen Ron in his office today, sleeves rolled up in an affected display of weekend casualness. Even though it was inconceivable that he could hear her from three doors down, she projected her voice. Showing him that she had not violated one of the (178, as it turned out), "Rooooles of Conduct for Contract Workers," which stipulated that any touching of clients had to be appropriate. She still couldn't believe he'd hired her. Maybe their shared experience with the elderly had been the clincher. Apparently the Lung Association had given her a glowing reference.

"Are you OK with a touch assist, Sunshine?" she asked again. Her head dangling about her knees, Sunshine nodded her assent. Janet brought her hand to the small of her back, and gently pressed it forward. "Try to bring your stomach up just a little bit so you don't strain your back ... just a teeny bit more ... perfect!"

Going from girl to girl, with the merest brush of her fingertips, she realigned a spine, adjusted a shoulder, guided them deeper into the pose. Rules aside, she was also sensitive to the fact that for most of these girls, at some point, touch from an adult had been inappropriate, which had likely landed half of them on the street in the first place.

At the end of the hour, the girls were lying on their backs in the cool-down position, their abdomens rising and falling in a regular rhythm—a peaceful sight that Ron took in when he stopped to watch at the gym door window, then knocked.

"How's it going, Janet?" he whispered.

"Goooood. And you? Get caught up on your work?"

Now that she was on the team "(The Home Team" as she noticed some of the staff put it), he was slightly less reserved around her, and attempted a jocular shrug. "I wish," he said, indicating his briefcase. "More paperwork to finish up at home this weekend. It never ends around here."

With you, I bet it never will, she thought. But gratitude, a small starburst of shy pride in belonging, flared in her belly, and she found herself genuinely wishing him a nice weekend.

* * *

Her Saturdays fell into a happy routine—The Home, then off to the Y for her class for her senior patients. Ron was usually hunched over some manual when she passed his office, but his presence didn't inhibit her as much anymore. All her students were still showing up, which was gratifying, because sustaining interest with kids from such chaotic backgrounds was always tough. With her confidence boosted, she felt more comfortable talking to the girls about the psychological underpinnings of yoga, how it affected both the mind and body.

This morning, she had put them through a vigorous set of postures designed to free energy that was trapped in tense muscles, and now led them into the child's posture, or *bala*.

The girls folded into the pose, chests pressed to their thighs, foreheads on the floor, arms lying limply at their sides. Anyone looking in would think they were genuflecting before her, but it was much deeper than that. The child's posture was an intensely vulnerable posture, resembling the embryonic position first experienced in the womb, what was known as a "submissive" posture of letting go, opening the heart area.

Her throat caught as she looked at the girls curled up like armadillos, not one of them able to fully let go, every back arched up just a fraction too high.

"I'm going to give some of you a little touch assist to help you soften into the posture."

Shoulder blades, spinal muscles all tensed to varying degrees against her fingertips, which barely exerted any pressure at all. She didn't push it. It was not to be messed with, the fragile hold of the body-mind. What the mind couldn't bear, the body contained. It was during moments like this, when the girls were quiet, temporarily at peace, that they were the most vulnerable. Freed from their cellular cage of defensive anger, suppressed memories and emotions were likely to float up. And not just the proverbial repressed memory of your stepfather creeping into your bed. But softer, gentler, inarticulate emotions related to love. A vague and almost unbearable awareness of the pure, decent sort of love that existed in the world, and the grievous sense of injury of being cheated out of that.

The CD stopped, filling the room with a hallowed quiet. Dangerous, yes, to try to release those buried emotions, but even more dangerous to keep them in the shadows, forever unnamed and unexpressed.

She kept her voice soft, so very soft, just like her fingertips. A whisper, featherweight, barely audible.

"Often when we have bad or hurtful memories that the mind can't accept, they're stored in the body. Your body is in a safe place now. Listen to your body, and let those feelings float up, even if they are painful. And know that there is wisdom in your body, too. What is your body trying to tell you?"

Hers was telling her that she was becoming attracted to one of her students. Angela Hubert. Twenty or so, with a heart-shaped face, porcelain skin, and a gush of jet-black hair swept up into an exuberant ponytail. Angela was one of those chronically late students, bursting into class a few minutes after it started with a laughing "Sorry, sorry, sorry!!" But she made up for it with the intensity of her attention. Sitting perfectly still in the lotus position, she had a way of listening with utter raptness, as if her very pores were trying to absorb everything Janet said. At first, Janet didn't see her as anything other than a high-spirited girl whose attentiveness was gratifying. But when one day she suddenly felt self-conscious adjusting Angela's elbow, she knew something had shifted.

One morning after class, Angela stayed behind. It was the first weekend in October, sunny and warm after a week of rain. Ron had finally taken the Saturday off, making an ostentatious point of it by hanging a goofy "Gone fishing!" sign on his office door. Usually after class, a few of the girls hung around to talk to Janet—especially Sunshine, who liked to recount her latest bout of allergies. But with today's good weather, they'd all streamed out en masse after class, leaving her alone with Angela.

She remained on her back on the mat in the cool-down pose, her eyes closed. Absolutely still, except for her flat, almost concave belly which was rising and falling in even rhythm under the loose pink T-shirt she wore with a pair of black, low-rise yoga pants. Janet stood over her, watching her breath deepen, wondering if she had fallen asleep. But then Angela's eyes popped open and she broke into a wide smile.

"Oh man, this is just what I needed," she said. "I was out at this club all night. Just grabbed a coffee this morning, and came down here."

And you're *telling* me this, Janet thought. Knowing I could report you to Ron for violating god knows what rules of conduct you girls have to abide by—the size of a telephone book compared to hers. Surely The Home had some sort of curfew! Momentarily too flustered to speak, she distracted herself by straightening up the mats in the storage drawers. When she turned around again, Angela was still lying on her back, eyes closed, submerged in her stage of bliss. Janet stopped a few feet away from her mat.

"So, you're feeling good now?" she asked.

"A-MAZ-ING!!! Like this total calm." Angela opened her eyes again and gazed up at the bare ceiling as if it were the Sistine Chapel. "Except that now I want to fuck it up."

Janet laughed. "What do you mean?"

"I dunno. It feels weird to be this calm. It doesn't feel

natural. Now, I dunno ... I want to kick over a garbage can or something."

Bright sunlight poured through the small upper window of the gym. For the first time, Janet noticed how high Angela's forehead was in profile, how the light caught the curve of it, highlighting it like a cupped hand.

She clasped her own hands behind her back. "I used to feel like that before I met my husband Daniel. I was filled with this wild, self-destructive energy, and I didn't know where it would take me."

"Yeah, and your friends are like ... oh, oh! Stay away from her, today!"

"But after doing yoga for a while, I found that I became more addicted to feelings of peace rather than chaos, if you know what I mean. Doing it consistently really does produce biochemical changes in your body, and you start to honour that calm space within you."

Especially when you've been scared shitless by where the chaotic energy could take you. It was the turning point in her life, waking up in a Bangkok hotel room with her ex-boyfriend and the rich German businessman they had met the night before. She wasn't sure how she'd gotten there, but that wasn't unusual in those days. Waking up wasted, feeling the petri dish of various ejaculatory fluids fermenting in her vagina. On the other side of the bed, lay a frightened Thai girl, who Janet vaguely recalled had joined them last evening. Unbearably young in the sober light of morning, maybe not even 14. Careful not to wake the men, the girl mince-stepped with stilted formality to the washroom, her anus clotted with dark blood. *They had done that to her? While she, Janet, was in the room with her, passed out?*

Fortunately, her boyfriend and the German were still deep in drugged sleep, which made it easy for Janet to pick through their wallets and distribute the bulk of what amounted to a considerable amount of money to the Thai girl, leaving some for herself. Up to then, she had lived solely in the short term, her future dictated by where her boyfriend wanted to go next. But she had heard about the transporting qualities of yoga, which had yet to become mainstream, of gurus perched in mysterious mountain retreats. That morning, she was on a train, headed to the ashram in the foothills of the Himalayas where she would meet Daniel.

"So what I need is discipline, right?" Angela said.

"I don't really like that word. I prefer to say commitment. You don't need a big space to do yoga. You can do it in your room. Any quiet place."

"That's not going to happen there. My roommates are noisy."

"You can do yoga anywhere. A beach. A park."

Angela considered this, shifting onto her side so she could look directly at Janet. Her T-shirt slipped up, exposing a bare strip of lower belly. Plush, despite her thinness, as if a fine layer of a pearly substance—not quite fat, not quite cream—had been injected just under her skin.

She suddenly sat up. "Hey! Am I keeping you from something?"

"No ... well, I do have another class at 12:30."

"Sorry! I didn't mean to take up your time."

"No! Not at all!"

While Janet put away her mat, Angela pulled on a pair of black sneakers, and grabbed her grey hoodie that had been lying against the wall. Then she waited for Janet to fill out the attendance form, and fell in alongside her as they headed down the empty hall.

No one was around, and the corridors gave off the vast ringing emptiness of a high school in summer. Walking past Ron's closed door, with its silly sign, Janet felt the strangeness of not being under his constant surveillance, imagined or otherwise. She kept her gaze on the new posters on the walls. The Home Halloween bash, with a prize for the best mask! At the end of the hall, a flight of stairs led up to the dorm, where she assumed Angela would head to sleep off her night of partying. But she followed her out into the empty courtyard.

"So what are you up to today?" Janet asked.

"Not much. Just meeting a friend."

Janet jiggled her car keys in her palm. Where was everybody? Even the cramped Victorian houses across the street looked deserted, as if their occupants had bolted off to the beach or cottage to enjoy what might be the last warm day of the year. Above the rooftops, banks of brilliantly white cumulus clouds piled up, cordoning off the area.

"Can I give you a lift anywhere? I'm going to the Annex."

"Are you passing Christie Park?"

"As a matter of fact, I'm driving right past there."

"Cool!"

Angela's nearness, her faint sweaty smell, made the inside of her car more buglike. What's the big deal Janet argued with herself. She was only giving the girl a ride. Had it been pouring rain, she wouldn't have thought twice about giving any of these girls a lift if it were on her way. Besides, they certainly weren't *touching*.

To guarantee that, Janet kept her hands hitched up

high on the steering wheel, her right elbow crooked inward to avoid grazing Angela's knee, which was pointed toward her, joggling to some inner music. Nonetheless, she felt paranoid turning onto Bloor, half-expecting Ron to pull up alongside, in full fisherman regalia.

"So Angela, are you originally from Toronto?" she asked, aiming for a generic conversation.

"No, I'm a Newfie. From a place called Gander. Ever heard of it?"

A small thrill went up Janet's spine. "Heard of it? I used to live there when I was a teenager! My father was posted on a military base there!"

Angela's smile split her face. "Git out of here!"

"No, I did!"

Janet usually liked to get to her seniors' class early, to spend a few moments focusing her energy for her elderly patients, who were touch-deprived and heartbreakingly grateful for the slightest bit of attention. But now her heart leapt when she saw a construction roadblock ahead that would allow her to stretch out her time with Angela, who was rocking back and forth, clapping her hands together as if she had just seen an amazing magic trick.

"You lived in Gander? I don't believe it! I don't fucking believe it! When did you live there?"

"Oh ... probably long before you were born." She paused, deciding that to give any hint of appearing younger was pathetic. "In the 70s."

"AMAZING!! What was it like back then?"

"I don't know. What's it like now?"

"Boring."

"Well, that's what it was like back then."

Angela let out another whoop of laughter and slapped her knees. Unfuckingbelievable!!! Last night, no, wait, it was the night before, she met this guy from Gander at a club, wasn't that wild? Janet smiled, feeling a sudden spasm of jealousy for this unknown guy who had been close to Angela. At Ossington, she purposely slowed down, even though the construction had cleared. Usually she found this strip of street depressing, with its old, run-down brick buildings given over to dollar stores. But now it was as if the clear fall air had sandblasted each and every building, de-lineating neglected details of interlocking brickwork with elegant art deco cornices in the upper stories.

Christie Park appeared all too soon, a neon green bil-liard table, flanked by trees blazing in full autumn foliage. The park was crowded: dog walkers, a man doing tai chi, couples sprawled on benches.

"Anywhere in particular you want to be dropped off?"

"Nope. Here is good."

Janet pulled up to the curb.

"Is your friend here?"

"No, but they're never on time anyway." Angela pointed to a tree in the centre of the park, the illuminated umbrella of a canary-yellow elm. "Maybe I'll just crash under that tree and wait."

Crash? Kids still used that antiquated 70s expression? Janet wanted to utter something cautionary, but a car honked behind her. Angela opened the door and jumped out.

"Hey! Thanks so much for the ride!"

"You take care now."

"I will."

She arrived ten minutes late for her seniors' class, feeling guilty at their abandoned looking faces as they buzzed toward her, eager to explain the various physical ailments that she would have to honour today. Shamefully, she rushed them through their poses and, when the class was finished, bolted to her car. She practically drove through a red light getting back to Christie Park. But each subsequent drive around the park revealed no girl with a jutting ponytail curled up under a tree, laughing uproariously with the friend she was supposed to meet.

* * *

"You might want to be careful with this Angela person," Daniel said out of the blue one night before dinner.

"What do you mean?"

"I mean, you are a very intense person when you're aroused, and you don't always realize the intensity of your drive."

"Oh, thank you very much! Thanks for thinking I'm so stupid I don't know what's appropriate! You're right! The next time she comes to class, I'm going to jump her!"

"Janet—I'm just saying, be careful. You really don't know this girl."

"And you don't either, so fuck off!"

After a silent supper, she went over to him and kneaded his shoulders while he was washing the dishes. "I'm concerned about her, that's all. She's staying out all night. I don't want her to get kicked out of The Home."

"She knows the rules. It's not your problem."

She watched him dry a copper bowl they'd bought in India, which they used for serving rice.

"Do you think I'm becoming a little too hung up on this girl?"

"I do."

"How can you tell?"

He looked away from her with a pained smile. "You remind me of the way I was when I first met you."

* * *

What keeps her awake at night—or, alternatively, sleeping for 15 hours straight—are thoughts of how deeply she hurt Daniel. She had assumed, despite his reservations, that it was a turn-on for him too. Sharing fantasies, having the occasional threesome, had been part of their sex life, and she was unapologetic about her infatuation, even indulged it, because it was never going to go beyond that. Wanting someone she couldn't have was new to her. Wasn't infatuation, kept within strict bounds, like any sensual pleasure, something to savour? *A treat?* She began to crave the build-up of anticipation, the way it made her feel alive, a natural, harmless high with a reckless edge that felt in character for her.

One touch. She only allowed herself to give Angela *one* touch assist per class. One chaste, seemingly casual, intoxicating, premeditated touch to align her in position, barely permitting her pulsing fingertips to graze her skin. Afterward, Daniel would be the recipient of her pent-up passion, forging, what she truly believed then, was complicity with her fantasy.

* * *

Every week Janet had a theme for her class; this day's was "Staying Centred through a Transition." It was something she'd given a lot of thought to, because coming from a sheltered environment, or "reintegrating into society" as they put it at The Home, could be a bewildering experience for some. After being a victim for so long, shedding that old skin, and thickening a new one could be daunting, sending the more vulnerable girls skidding back to their old familiar habits when things didn't work out.

"Is everyone here?" she asked as the clock indicated eleven.

She meant Angela of course, who had yet to arrive. Only eight girls had shown up, including Sunshine, who had a wad of tissue balled in one hand, into which she continually sniffed. Janet turned on her CD player, starting a homemade compilation of tranquillity music mixed with ocean sounds, which she thought that Angela, being an ex-Maritimer, would like. Probably on the streetcar at this very moment, rushing back from a night of clubbing. "Sorry! Sorry! Sorry!" she would say, bounding into the room, her ponytail bobbing behind her endearingly bulging forehead.

At five minutes after eleven, Janet positioned herself at the front of the class, and brought her fingers to the sides of her torso.

"Today, we're going to focus on the manipura, our core chakra. That's our solar plexus area, which includes our abdominal muscles, and the breathing muscles in our diaphragm. Not only are these muscles important because they support us, but a strong centre also supports us psychologically. In yoga, this is called the power centre, the centre of strength and self worth." She tapped her sides, which were still, even in her forties, drum-tight. "The way you think about yourself, the way you let others treat you ... it all comes from here. Your core."

Sunshine honked loudly into her tissue.

"Are you OK, Sunshine? Do you have a cold?"

"No," she said grumpily. "I'm allergic to the glue from the masks they made at the Halloween party."

Allergic to anyone trying to have a good time you mean, Janet thought, as Kalea, another chronic latecomer, straggled in and set up her mat. From down the hallway, she heard a high peel of laughter too shrill to be Angela's.

"Is anyone else coming, Kalea? No? OK, I guess we'd better start. Now in these poses, we want to be aware of keeping our abdominal muscles really, really strong. Sometimes when we do the poses, I ask you to keep a soft stomach, but in these, I really want you to concentrate on keeping your stomach muscles tight? OK? So let's begin with The Warrior."

Forty-five minutes later, the girls were bowed into the child's pose, lulled into deep relaxation by the muscle stretches and the music. The soft rush of surf sounds blended with the gentle swish of the breeze strumming the trees outside—a symphonic mist of synthetic and natural sound, which Janet would have dissolved into, were she not compulsively still glancing at the gym door.

Sunshine had stopped sniffling, although her back was still hoisted up too high, jutting up like an embankment on her broad thighs. Kneeling behind her, Janet placed the back of her palms on the swelling top of her haunches. No wonder she had back problems. She was carrying so much weight, her flesh flabby as an old woman's, that the underlying muscular padding was dense with blocked energy.

In contrast, Angela had tiny buttocks, dainty as china teacups, her tailbone curving elegantly into the smudged shadow of a crease barely discernible above the band of her yoga pants. When Janet assisted her in this pose (that one carefully allocated touch!), she didn't dare press the backs of her palms into her lower back as she was doing with Sunshine, because if her hands were to slip *down there*—

"Just relax and take long, deep exhalations, OK?"

Her heart did its foolish leap when she heard footsteps approaching, but it was only Ron, glancing at the class, then giving her a brusque, friendly nod before setting off. She glided her hands up toward Sunshine's shoulder blades, feeling more muscular resistance under the padding, what William Reich had called "body armour." Janet saw it as tiny muscle fibres literally seizing up against the continued assault of childhood abuse, both physical and verbal, and visualized her palm as a warm iron, steaming out the pleats and creases of deeply embedded trauma.

"Let me know if this hurts, Sunshine."

Sunshine's voice came from a congested nasal cavity. "So far it feels all right."

"You may have a runny nose for the next few days, but it's not necessarily your allergies. What I'm doing now releases a lot of emotional energy, so it could be one of the blocks clearing itself out, and ... oh my god, it's ten after twelve! We've run over!"

Kalea came up to her as she filled out the attendance form. "That was awesome! I'm so glad I came!" she said.

"Thank you, Kalea. Where is everyone today? Have some of the girls left town?"

Kalea shrugged. "I saw Angela in bed this morning. She was still sleeping. But I don't know about the others."

*　*　*

"Is everyone here?" she asked the following Saturday. After a month of Indian summer, fall had rushed in with a vengeance; trees bathed in a soft Pernod glow of lush foliage one day, whipped bare the next. The near-empty gym spread out before her as dank and dreary looking as an airplane hangar, cold drizzle stippling the window.

She clicked on her CD of ocean sounds. Stupid thinking Angela would show up. Why wouldn't she stay in bed? Resolve dissolved on days like this, draining out any promise. This type of weather was the worst for Janet, tossing her back on moods she tried so hard to rise above.

"So that's it? Just three today?" Kalea, Dalea, and of course, Sunshine, looking absolutely radiant in an ensemble of T-shirt and sweatpants in pick-me-up shades of cold wet cement and frozen sludge. "OK, we're still going to focus on strengthening our core muscles today, so let's start with The Warrior."

Another gust of wind, like scissors snipping each and every leaf into confetti, as if an edict had been issued to eradicate all colour. Janet could feel a prickly dullness falling over her that wasn't merely Angela's absence. Passing Ron's office earlier this morning, seeing him writing something, she had stopped to ask how he was doing. More preoccupied than usual, he had kept writing, his voice terse, as if it pained him to parse out his precious, limited moments to talk to the likes of her. "This job keeps growing more parts," he said. "I'm in the process of hiring new counsellors."

New counsellors. Why he might even be interviewing one of them right now. A proper young woman, from a proper family, with a proper degree, studded with the golden nuggets of volunteer work: shelters, food banks, literacy programs. Do-gooders out to do good in the world, and certainly doing better than her.

That was supposed to be me, she thought. Over 20 years ago, convinced of her special insight into troubled girls, she had fully expected to be counselling one day—or even running a house like this one.

"Move your foot a little, Sunshine, so you don't strain your knee. And move your left hip forward ... Yes ... like that, so you're standing squarely in the position."

Her spirits sank, making her feel more insignificant and marginalized. What did it take to teach yoga, anyway? Nothing. Anyone could staple a poster onto a telephone pole, alongside the offers for dog walking, babysitting services and guitar lessons from failed musicians.

You'd think, knowing her experience on the streets, that Ron would have asked for her input on something—just once.

Too stoopid to be part of the team. Too stoopid to be taken seriously or have anyone ask your opinion, what she thought of their rooools and tooools for re-integration. And look! Her students abandoning ship, the leaky vessel of her accumulated life's wisdom! Obviously they weren't dependent on her for their infusions of self worth!

She had prepared, for the cool-down, the proverbial white-light-dissolving-all-blocks visualization, which she didn't have the heart for now. But lacking the energy to come up with anything better, she trotted it out, thinking she sounded exactly like a small town minister with his little homilies—*Let a smile be your umbrella!*

"It was a good class today," Sunshine said afterward, rolling up her mat.

Janet stiffened. Had it come to this, Sunshine mocking her New Age earnestness? But she looked sincere enough, her thin lips turned up in an amiable smile, holding her shoulders in a more relaxed way than Janet had ever seen her exhibit, as if her armpits weren't sticky with glue.

"I'm glad you liked it. The core exercises are really important for building inner strength."

Sunshine widened her eyes, and jumped into a mock kung fu stance.

"I feel more empowered already! Invincible! Ready to take on the world!"

Janet laughed. It never occurred to her that the girl had a sense of humour. Sunshine was standing close to her, and for the first time Janet saw that her eyes were not puddle brown after all, but hazel, with a shot of chartreuse around the iris.

"No, seriously," Sunshine said. "I've really liked this set of exercises we've been doing for the past two weeks. They've really helped my back."

"Yes, I can see you're holding yourself better."

"I can sit for longer periods of time without it getting sore, and that's good because I want to go back to school in the new year."

"You're going back to school? What are you taking?"

Sunshine jumped back into her mock kung fu pose. "I'm going to be a legal assistant! I'm going to keep those lawyers honest!" She became serious again. "I was supposed to finish at Humber last year, but I had a few … setbacks and ended up here. I have to increase my class load if I want to graduate next year, and I was worried that I wouldn't be able to sit through the classes ... but maybe I'll be OK now."

Great gusts of air left Janet's lungs, as if they were rubber rafts being deflated. College degree? How she had misjudged this girl. The sullenness, she could see now, was a kind of stolidness, an old-fashioned forbearance in times of adversity. She could almost see Sunshine as a throwback to another time, her parent's generation: heading the Ladies Auxiliary, her stout figure flattered by a tweed suit worn with a lapel brooch, her name Myrtle instead of Sunshine, respected by all.

Choking up, she turned back to the attendance forms. This was the second to last class before her contract was renewed, and it looked like this girl, the one she had privately disparaged the most, would probably give her the best recommendation.

"Get your degree Sunshine. Pieces of paper are important."

* * *

On the last class of the year, she fully expected only Sunshine to show up. Passing Ron's office, she was relieved to see that he wasn't here to witness her failure. "Don't be so hard on yourself. Most of the girls appreciate you, and will be back again," Daniel had said, and he was right. At quarter to eleven, they bounced in en mass—*GaelaDaleaKalea!*—the original 15 from the looks of it, bombarding her with excuses for their absence—apparently the stomach flu had been going around The Home.

In her relief at seeing everyone again, Janet almost

didn't register Angela trailing behind the pack. She grabbed a mat, unrolled it beside Sunshine in the left corner, and flopped down on her back, her ponytail sprawled out behind her. No "sorry, sorry, sorry's," or any other acknowledgements of Janet.

"OK. It's good to see you all back again," she said, after everyone had arranged their mats in neat rows. "So let's start by lying on our backs in the savasana pose, and closing our eyes while we take deep breaths."

Having everyone close their eyes was a ploy so they wouldn't see her heading over to Angela, her own breath careening wildly in her rib cage. A few feet from Angela's mat, she stopped, wondering if the attraction, which had first revitalized, and then shamed her, was still there. Sickeningly, it was.

But it wasn't the same girl from a month ago. Something was off: her hair less glossy, her tiny body submerged in a pair of bulky grey sweatpants worn with a black, oversized Guns N' Roses T-shirt with jaggedly cut off sleeves. Janet didn't know what kids were listening to these days, but this rock band struck her as out of date. An angry guy's T-shirt.

Her voice quavered, as if it had been flung by a slingshot out of her mouth. "Now I want you to open your eyes and slowly sit up into a lotus position."

Angela rolled into the pose correctly, and gazed ahead. Nothing, not even a wisp of that intoxicatingly rapt attention. There was an indifference that would have seemed taunting, were it not so oblivious—making it perfectly apparent that she had only shown up so she could garner the requisite points for participation in an activity, a big deal at The Home.

Sunshine, slumped on the mat beside Angela, offered Janet the convenient diversion of poor posture. After adjusting her torso in a show of concern, she turned to Angela and nonchalantly asked: "How are you feeling today? You seem a little tired."

"No, I feel good. Peaceful," she shrugged.

So peaceful I want to fuck it up!

Then Janet saw the bruise. Yes, it was definitely the remnants of a fading bruise, that chalky ochre-yellow ring encircling Angela's upper left arm. A handprint from someone grabbing her—the owner of the Guns N' Roses T shirt, she'd be willing to bet, the guy from Gander. The kind of guy Janet had grown up with. A small town loser-boy who couldn't make it in the big city, stubbornly clinging to hard rock bands that no one listened to anymore, his hard luck stories and his victim's sense of entitlement. Had he grabbed her like that when she didn't bring him his beer fast enough? Or had Angela developed a taste for rough sex, quite enjoying "being hurt in a good way?"

She felt a rush to her head, a surge of honourable rage, her *raison d'être* for being here. Almost giddy now, she returned to the front of the class.

"Today we're going to spend time doing the poses that activate the root chakra, which is in your pelvic area, at the base of your spine. In women, this is a very powerful centre that is the source of your sexuality and creativity, but it can be affected by upheavals and abuse in our life. When the energy gets trapped there, it can weaken us."

And every mean man will sense it, she wanted to say. Under your tough talk, your tattoos, your cultivated swearing, they'll know that you can be pushed around. Just like I was before I met my husband, because that's the only way a guy can control you, make you feel inferior. And that man's child will grow in your belly, if you're not careful. And you will likely have to raise it on your own. And you will turn into your mother, your father, the very person you swore you'd never be and ran away from. And I don't care if I don't have a fancy piece of paper to back it up because I know it to be true!

"So now, let's do some exercises to help release that negative energy."

She instructed them to do standing squats first, keeping their abdominal muscles tight. Out of the corner of her eye, she saw Ron watching her through the gym door window, apparently working today after all. She gave him an ingratiating wave, thinking it was imperative now that her contract be renewed, that she be allowed more time with these girls.

"Sunshine, keep your stomach in, OK? It's bulging out a little. We don't want a soft stomach in this pose. We want a hard stomach. Squeeze, *squeeze* those abdominals."

Briefly returning her wave, Ron headed down the hall. Janet instructed the girls to go into the bridge, a backbend of sorts with the hands supporting the lower spine as it curved up into an arc.

"This is a very powerful posture that acts like a bridge from your base chakra to your heart chakra. It can be hard on the back, so I want you to rise up very slowly."

All the girls raised their hips obediently, including Angela, whose knees were splayed out a little too wide, giving Janet a legitimate excuse to go over and give her a touch assist. That touch. That one carefully allocated touch, which was abhorrent to her now, yet so necessary as well. That was the worst thing—she had witnessed harm coming to this girl, she would do anything to protect her, yet at the same time she felt the longing.

The sick ritualization took over. The measured walk. The pulsing fingertips curled into loose fists behind her back. When she was a couple of feet away from Angela, she stopped. The turmoil of conflicting emotions, those rigorously contained desires crackled through her, making her feel like some demented, electrified totem pole about to crash down on the girl. With a titanic effort to be natural, she knelt down beside Angela, carefully bringing her hands down inches away from her hips.

"Angela, you're too ..." she began. Then she saw another set of hips ramping up beside Angela's, a stockier set, which couldn't support the weight of the angle it was straining toward. "No, Sunshine! You're going to hurt your back doing that. Your balance is off ..."

But it was Angela's balance that was off. Just as Janet was reaching over to grab Sunshine, Angela toppled sideways, causing Janet's hands, for a split, horrible second before she yanked them back, to wind up deep in Angela's crotch.

"Holy shit!" Angela cried, jumping up.

"I'm sorry, Angela! I am so sorry! That was not intentional!"

But Angela kept brushing at her upper thighs as if trying to get rid of tiny gnats. "Jesus Christ, man! Your hands were *hot*!"

* * *

Ron's office seemed larger than the last time she had been in it, still packed with its towerscape of manuals, but with a spaciousness to it, as if his efforts to improve The Home were amplifying the very dimensions of the room. When he brusquely asked her to sit down in the chair across from his desk, she mutely complied. They were silent for a few moments as he flipped through a manual before him, the one with the royal blue cover, which she knew was *that* manual. Not the rooooooles anymore, but the rules, a set of fundamental, decent guidelines designed to protect the weak. Almost dizzy with shame and anxiety, she clutched her hands in her lap, and watched as Ron stopped right where she knew he would, at a page near the centre of the manual.

"I'm going to cut to the chase here, Janet. I'm afraid one of our clients have registered a complaint against you."

She nodded, numb. Lying awake half the night, she wondered how Angela would have told him. Had she flown into his office in an indignant rage, demanding that he fire the old perv? Or had she been crying, traumatized, her trust in people—all those so-called caring adults with their hidden, sleazy agendas—broken? Giving her one more reason to harden herself against the world, to cling to her abusive, hard-done-by boyfriend.

"Sunshine Roberts registered the complaint."

Sunshine? Yes, well that made sense, didn't it? The physically unfavoured, hypersensitive to all the increments of attention that had been withheld from birth. Likely observing Janet's infatuation from the moment she had made her first calculated step toward Angela, culminating in witnessing her fervid pawing of Angela's crotch.

"She said you told her she was fat."

"Pardon?"

"You told Sunshine she was fat."

"*Fat?*"

"She said you made disparaging comments about her weight more than once. Apparently you told her right in front of the other girls that her stomach was hanging out." He brought his finger down to a line near the bottom of the page. "That's a direct violation of rule 73, which states that all part-time personnel interacting with clients will speak to them in a respectful, supportive manner."

"But I ..."

Completely thrown, Janet could only stare at the manual. Then she remembered the standing squatting pose, her gentle admonition to Sunshine.

"But ... I said *soft* stomach! That's a yoga term! Some poses are done with a hard or soft belly. It's a common expression! Teachers use it all the time!"

Ron frowned. "Yes, I understand that, Janet. But when I observed your class last Saturday, you appeared to be singling Sunshine out, telling her to pull in her stomach ..."

"That's because she has back problems! These poses have to be done correctly or you can pull a muscle! I was concerned with her posture!"

To her surprise, Ron grinned and shook his head with exasperated relief.

"You know, Janet, I believe you. It's not our policy to give out personal information about our clients, but I will tell you that Sunshine has issues about her weight. Her mother was a well-known fashion model and one of the reasons Sunshine left home was because she felt she was being judged on how she looked. With all due respect, that young woman can be a little ... *challenging.*"

"Did anyone else make a complaint against me?"

"No, on the whole, the comments on your class were very favourable. I really think the girls got something out of your class, Janet—which isn't something I can say about most of our activities." Frowning again, he drummed the open manual with his fingers. "But unfortunately, Sunshine did issue a formal complaint, which I have to acknowledge. So, tell you what, Janet—your contract will definitely be renewed for next year, but I have to put you on three months probation."

"Probation?"

"Look, I know it sounds a little draconian, but it's just a formality, the way we do things around here, and ..."—he made a sweeping gesture toward the manuals to make light of it all—"I don't like it either! It just means more paper-work for me, filing yet another report."

In an instant Janet was up, galvanized by a jolting pain that went through her thigh as her knee slammed against the inner corner of his desk.

"Then let me just take that off your plate, Ron. I quit."

* * *

When the fog used to roll in around Gander, it was at first deceptively playful. There it would be, a bright, sunny blue-sky day, and then wafts of tissue-y mist that would suddenly appear, elongating into soft white scarves which would gently snake around your wrists, your ankles, your face until you were completely mummified, engulfed in a terrifying lack of visibility. In Toronto that winter, the fog offered no teasing preamble, but merely hung in a persistent gray drizzle that refused to crystallize into snow. Merging dark sky and dark, wet cement and giving a dark cast to the bed sheets as she woke up every morning beside Daniel.

"Where are you going?" he'd ask when she requested the car keys.

"Out. I need some space."

Her first stop, because it was near their apartment, was the methadone clinic on Dufferin Street. Slowing down to scan the bodies huddled on the sidewalk, zooming in on the bad-ass guys with their girlfriends freezing their tiny, tea-cup asses in tight jeans and short leather jackets, none of them Angela. After that she'd cruise one transitional neighbourhood after another until she came to Christie Park.

Most days, there was a place to park on the eastern side, where she could get a fairly long view of the comings and goings. What irrational urge prompted her to think that Angela might come here? A hunch, that's all. Rural Newfies tended to be creatures of habit, and if they found a place they liked to hang out in they were likely to stick to it.

"Why didn't you rat on me?" was the first question she'd ask Angela. So many brownie points in being the aggrieved victim, which Angela could have milked for all they were worth. Being groped by Janet might even have erased any demerit points she'd accumulated for sneaking out. Ferreted out extra care from the staff, because they failed to sufficiently protect her from the lecherous yoga teacher. Another black mark against spiritual healers—she was right up there with pervy priests with her diddling "touch assists."

With the miserable weather, the trees stripped bare, the remaining die-hard leaves pitchforked onto spikey branches, the park was mostly deserted. Through her cloudy windshield, she'd watch the odd person hustling through the park, seeking shelter, and imagine that she was talking to Angela in the relatively cozy confines of her Beetle. Janet would buy her something warm and nourishing—a creamy cappuccino, a nutty biscotto. While Angela talked, Janet would scan her neck for the mottled blossoms of fading bruises. And, of course, she wouldn't even think of touching the girl, for that sad infatuation, which had got her to this place, was on its way to petering out.

Every now and then she would see some poor soul enter the park, sink onto a wet bench, and stay there: knowing it probably wasn't good for them to be sitting in the cold, but unable to do anything but keep sitting there. Janet knew the feeling. Resolve dissolved on days like this, beached on the rocks of your continual ineptitude. But failure was familiar at least, so why budge? Around four, when the first of the regular dog walkers arrived, their Labs and Golden Retrievers tearing through the scrim of malaise with their pent-up, happy energy, she headed home.

* * *

"I think you should see a doctor," Daniel said.

"Oh, and you do, do you, Daniel. And why is that?"

"You're not handling things well."

"And how would you know that? How would you know that? Have you been following me?"

His face sunk turtle-like into his neck, suggesting that he had indeed borrowed a friend's car one afternoon, and trailed after her.

"You're the one who always handles things for me, aren't you? You're the one who's got his shit together. You're the one who *rescued* me, remember? Why don't you figure out how to handle this?"

She knew she was hurting him, but she couldn't stop it, the ugly, ballooning anger.

"Oh, I can't possibly do anything right for myself! Oh, I can't possibly think for myself! Oh, what should I do now, Daniel? Oh, what *shall* I do?"

* * *

Come January, there was still no snow, which would have at least brightened up the monotonous trudge of winter's gray plateau. Moreover, she received the bad news that due to reduced funding, there would be no more senior classes at the Y, her Saturday ritual.

No classes period, because she couldn't dredge up the energy to look for work. She kept searching for Angela, because it had become a ritual of sorts, getting out of the way of Daniel's scrutinizing, worried gaze, with him knowing there was no dealing with her when she got like this. A tired game between them, her becoming remote, out of reach, simultaneously pissing him off, turning him on. She had to punish him for her dependence on him, this latest failure one more example of how she probably couldn't survive without him. Stretch out this little meltdown, for the time would come, soon enough, when this grayness would seep into her like cement and he would have to get her out of bed, make sure she ate, send her off to her doctor for an antidepressant, and she would be grateful.

* * *

"Did you ever hitchhike in the fog, Angela?" she found herself asking her one afternoon during one of their imaginary conversations, where Angela was ensconced in the seat beside her, slapping her knees at the memory.

Funny how this Toronto drizzle, so insipid compared to Newfoundland's black-ice whiteouts, could throw her back on her teenage self. Days when she would hitchhike in zero visibility, risk getting picked up by a redneck who hated hippie girls, just to break the boredom. Or to get away from her father's ("that's Captain Pierce to you, stupid!") onslaught of insults, which had carved themselves into her psyche. Staying out all night because you might as well do something to earn the beatings when you got home.

Her thighs. He used to take the strap to the top of her thighs. The first girl ever to wear a miniskirt at her high school, her thicket of bruises would be on full display to the teacher and principal—but in those days, on a military base especially, it was normal to have strict parents. After one particularly harsh beating, which her mother, the upright captain's wife, barely blinked through, she left home.

But what about the other significant home in her life, which she had, as she could see now, so foolishly left?

In a masochistic change of pace, she abandoned her perch at the park one afternoon and headed down to The Home. That afternoon a herd of clouds had threatened to turn into a downpour, but a section of sky had cleared around The Home, bathing its bricks in a sienna glow. The first thing she saw as she parked a block away was the sign saying that The Home facilities would be expanded in the new year, the empty warehouse next door marked for renovation. As if on cue, Ron emerged from the front door with what could only be his new counsellor, a young, generic preppie blonde who was smiling at something he said. They wore matching dark overcoats with collegiate looking tartan scarves wrapped around their necks. All that was missing were the pompoms. "Yay, Home Team!" Doing very well—extremely well without the likes of her. Watching the two cross the street with the easy companionability of colleagues, she wondered if they had hired a new yoga teacher yet. Perhaps Ron had just spotted some tattered sign on a post, and called. It was so easy to be replaced.

As she drove away, the heavens suddenly opened. Not a Toronto rain, but a Newfoundland one, lacerating her car with massive drops, instantly backing up the sewers. At Dufferin, one of her windshield wipers stopped, and when she pulled over to the sidewalk and opened her car door to fix it, a truck sped by, splashing her legs and front seat with icy water. Tears spurted from her eyes, the oceanic bath of self-pity. Then, through the streaming rain on her windshield, she saw another sign, this one in front of a tiny church, and she burst out laughing.

Let a smile be your umbrella.

Back at home, her home, in the calm, safe harbour of Daniel's unconditional love, she knew the spell had been broken. Laughter was the best medicine. And love. The love of a good man; something that so few were lucky to have. How horrible she had been to him over the past few months, but she would make it up to him now. Tonight she would surprise him with his favourite coconut curried lamb, served by candlelight on their nicest dishes.

"What's the matter?" she asked when he set down his fork after two bites.

"I don't know. I have this pain in my side."

She placed her palm flat on the area he indicated, and jerked her hand back again.

"Jesus Christ, Daniel! It feels like you're burning up inside! We have to get you to a doctor!

* * *

What should I do now, Daniel?

What should she do? And how long had she been sitting in her car, this stifling sanctuary, with her pitiful pile of flyers bleaching out in the back seat? Flyers that, a long time ago, this morning it was, she had intended to pin up in health food stores across the city. No place for them on bulletin boards anymore. No place anywhere for the likes of her. Far better for her to go home to the apartment they once shared, which she wasn't sure she could afford anymore, and collapse.

She headed west along Bloor, the humidity closing in. Such an ugly, congested part of the city with its strip clubs and dollar stores. Whereas the heat had expanded everything in Rosedale, here it squashed the huddled brick storefronts like a hostile hand, spewing cheap merchandise onto the sidewalk. And her, with the crotch of her biking shorts still moist from Steve's pool this morning, that mingled odour of drying chlorine and vaginal juices making her one with the squalid environment.

Would it have made any difference if Daniel had told me earlier? she had asked the doctor. Inoperable, he had replied. Nothing either of them could have done. *But I could have loved you better, watched you better, paid more attention, not automatically assumed that the grim worry that had descended upon you was because of me. So sorry, sorry, sorry.*

Halfway home on Bloor, her car stalled. She pulled the clutch, but could not bring this car to life.

In India, where they naively saw death as a passage, they viewed cremations as indifferently as they would a demolition crew. She remembered one picnic on the Ganges, watching while Hindu monks laid a body on a funeral pyre. It was one of those days that captured the quintessential spirituality of India; the monks regal in their maroon robes, the clouds high and luminous, the soul rising in a spire of sacred smoke, and settling into some celestial way station for its next incarnation.

How stupid she had been to cremate him here, disperse his ashes in Toronto. All these undeserving people breathing in what may be the last of his lingering precious particles. That mullet-haired meathead jerking the choke chain of his poor pit bull puppy. That hawk-nosed store owner presiding over his cheap carpet emporium. And that young man behind her in his red greaseball Camaro honking at her, and telling her to "move, move it lady!" All these people did not deserve to breathe in one bit of her beloved.

Her finger went up in the air, a monument of defiance. Screw you, you stupid assholes! If my car wants to die here, so be it!

But her car did not die right then. It lasted just long enough to take her back to Rosedale that night, to Steve's house. He was right; everyone seemed to have taken off to their cottage that weekend. Nearly every palatial house was vacant, a dense quietude had settled over the neighbourhood. She pulled into the curved driveway, long and winding from her perspective, as if she were gazing down at it from the moon. On his backyard patio, she stripped off the sports bra and biker shorts, which clung to her as if her sweat had woven them into her skin, and stood naked.

Quiet as a tomb, Steve had said, and as tombs went, it was lovely. Full moon. The pool shimmering in its shifting shapes, offering purification.

She slipped into the water. After Daniel's death, her doctor had given her a month's supply of sleeping pills. In a little while, she would decide whether to swallow all of them. For now, she would just float, sealing herself in that soothing membrane between coolness and the sweltering air, much like when they used to float in the Indian Ocean. Daniel, always the stronger swimmer, would swim out so far, his bronzed, bald head becoming a dot as he approached the horizon. I've lost him, she'd think when it would disappear altogether. But then it would reappear, his familiar features surfacing as he ploughed through the amplitude of turquoise sea, straight toward her.

Doughnut Eaters

⟡

Stepping out onto my front porch one night to take my dog out for his evening walk, I became transfixed by the sight of the man who lived across the street from me. He was heading to his car to pick up his teenaged daughter—something I knew he did regularly from one of the few pleasantries I had exchanged with his wife since moving to this new neighbourhood after my divorce three months earlier. Mist, thick from a day of solid drizzle, rose up from the sidewalks, blurring the brown-brick houses. Half a block away, they all dissolved into a long, black tunnel, giving the impression that this street—still unfamiliar to me, and empty except for this man and I—could lead anywhere.

He didn't see me on the porch, standing absolutely still, watching him. A tall, languid man in his mid-forties, he strolled to his car, one hand in the pocket of his khaki shorts, the other jiggling car keys. His head was lowered. Preoccupied, I wondered? Or with the affectionate, mock-exasperation of the duty-bound father?

An unexpected wave of bitter longing hit me. Mine had been a long, combative marriage, my emotions frozen to deal with my husband's hair trigger temper, a switchblade that could snap out at any time. My therapist had warned me that after I left my husband, and broke through the ice-hold of my defenses, other, long-buried emotions would well up. This would release the hurt of my damaged inner child, she explained, which made me feel like such a cliché that I stopped seeing her.

The man's car was parked on my side of the street, a few doors down from me. Why wasn't he glancing up at me, when surely he had to be aware of the intensity of my gaze, my whole being focused on him? "He never does things around the house, but he'll take the kids anywhere or pick them up," his wife had told me during one of our brief exchanges.

"My father never picked me up," I wanted to snap back. "In fact, I wouldn't have dared ask him because it wasn't allowed."

Wasn't *allowed*. Such a whiney voice in my head, such an aggrieved, hard done by voice. One that I held in check because I was turning 50 in a month, and was embarrassed to be dredging up childhood wounds. The admission also seemed so bizarre, an aberration of the natural father/daughter relationship that had set the embattled tone for my marriage, and would probably strike again when I became ready for another relationship.

Even if a marriage is only a shell, a shell still offers protection, I had written in my journal. And here I was, resentful for feeling stripped so bare, so suddenly and irrationally vulnerable, just by watching this man.

What would it feel like to be his daughter? To have love that you could never doubt? That was just *there*, like air?

That wouldn't be retracted if you did something wrong. Used the wrong tone of voice. Called him far too late, as this daughter had likely just done, *laughing*, daring to laugh at the inconvenience she was causing him by demanding, "Hey Dad. Can you pick me up?"

Still unaware of me, he inserted his key into the car door.

Look at me, I thought. See me. Walk towards me. Talk to me. Turn around.

But he didn't. And in his easy walk, that languid, mock-exasperated, put-upon father look, I saw all that had been denied me, all that would be denied. A naturally protective parental love, one that needed to be certain of a daughter's safety on a foggy night like this, when a person could suddenly dissolve into the blackness.

* * *

Mists wrapped themselves around the landscape of my childhood, a long-vanished rural Germany which was, in the mid-sixties, still reconstructing itself after the Second World War. My father was in the Canadian Air Force, part of the NATO alliance, an essential military presence necessitated by the Cold War threat. From the ages of seven to twelve, I lived in Hugelsheim, a small village in south-western Germany, about half a mile from the air force base where he was stationed. Everywhere, modern, industrialized towns were springing up, but Hugelsheim was plucked straight from a Breughel landscape. Horse-drawn carts clattering on cobblestone streets. Stork-y blond German boys in Lederhosen. And the church, with its high, Gothic spire, rising in the middle of town.

We—my father, mother, younger brother, and I—lived on Hauptstrasse, the main street, in an old, pre-war house. Like virtually every other home in the village, it was part of a working farm complex. Our front yard was no suburban green yard, but rather a long, rectangular strip of gravel with chicken coops on one side, and barns housing cows, haylofts and ancient, rusting farming implements on the other. No one we knew had a phone or a television set. Even the toilet in our shed-like bathroom was a luxury, for outhouses were still the norm in Hugelsheim, intensifying the smell of manure, which was omnipresent, permeating both the villages and the surrounding fields.

Our family was an anomaly, living off the air force base rather than in the Personal Military Quarters (PMQs) the other military families lived in. But then, my father wasn't like any of the other serviceman. He was Corporal Al Bracuk, former amateur lightweight boxing champion of Canada, once slated to fight Muhammad Ali—still known as Cassius Clay back then—in the 1960 Olympics. A tall, green-eyed blond who I once thought was the tiny golden boxer poised atop the boxing trophies in our house. "Big Al" denounced most of his fellow servicemen as sissies, who were dominated by their hen-pecking wives, and whose spoilt-rotten kids made demands that *his* kids knew we were not allowed to make.

Chief among his 'not alloweds' was eating anything made of white flour and sugar—candy, Wonder Bread, pastries, and most contemptible of all, *doughnuts*, a word he practically spat out. Instead we ate sandwiches made with wild honey and coarse pumpernickel bread purchased at the local German *gasthaus*. We were also not allowed to do poorly in school or sports, whine, complain, get sick, get fat, or ask him for a ride to and from the base unless it was offered. It was, after all, only about a mile away, and being his kids, *Big Al's kids*, we could easily walk or ride our bikes.

I've read somewhere that children are naturally conservative and don't like to be different. For us, there was little choice, because in post-war Germany of the mid-60s, even the most innocuous Canadian military family stood out with our fashionable clothes, new cars and prevailing patronizing attitude of having saved Europe from Hitler. Within that charmed bubble of being Canadian, there was a smaller one of being part of my family, a difference I luxuriated in, because to me, it meant being superior.

* * *

There is a black and white photo of us, the whole family at the Basel Zoo in 1965, swanning through a crowd of reserved Swiss. We are *Canadians*, the most stylish family these people have ever seen. Most of them are still dressed 20 years behind the times, the men wearing heavy formal jackets even in summer, the women in frumpy dirndl skirts. My father is ploughing ahead, as he always did on family outings, expecting us to blindly follow his lead. Which we are all doing without question, my mother tripping along by his side, my brother a few feet away from her, me taking up the rear.

In this photo a few of the European families have turned to stare shyly at us, something I was used to back then. Why wouldn't they? Look at my father, so smart in his Banlon sports shirt, front pleated pants, and shiny, leather dress shoes; my mother, so chic in an aqua shift dress made from the latest Butterick pattern; my brother, the all-Canadian boy in his Buster Brown shorts and T-shirt; and me, a 'swinging mod' in my lavender bellbottoms and matching pop top. I hold my ponytailed head high with the air of visiting royalty, knowing—even at my young age of ten—that I am privileged. Knowing that most Canadian kids weren't popping over to Switzerland for the weekends, nor did they have a handsome father who was a magnet for admiring glances, a father who would not turn around to acknowledge his family unless it was to tell them to hurry up.

And keep pace I did. I can see now in this photo that, like him, my gaze is tilted somewhere in the middle distance. I don't have to watch where he'll turn next as I can see my mother doing in this photo, her gay, tight public smile belying her constant anxiety about making him angry. I am pulled along by his momentum, his vast impatience to get to an exhibit he wants to see, the clip of his smart dress shoes on concrete creating a reverberating rhythm of urgency.

·That was me, a daughter who knew better than to treat her father like an ordinary man. Never asking him to slow down. Or begging for one of the slab-like Swiss chocolate bars beckoning everywhere from the kiosks designed like Alpine chalets. (Indeed, I had learned to avert my eyes quickly, even disdainfully, from chocolate bars I was not allowed to eat.) I am also aware that I am being stared at because I may be considered pretty. But without an idea of whether my father thinks I am (for I have been told that I don't look like him, that honour going to my milder natured, blonde, green-eyed brother of whom I'm jealous for that very reason), I can't be sure. But surely these people would see a similarity in my stride, the way I hold myself so straight, the way my brown hair shines because I only eat food that is good for me, because I am my father's daughter.

There is no photo of what happened to us after the zoo outing—getting lost on our way home. Apart from the major highways, European roads were not well marked in those days. Driving back to Germany from the Basel Zoo, my father missed a sign to the Autobahn, throwing us back into a rural Europe of the 19th century.

On this country road, where we found ourselves after dusk, there were no cars, no lights, no sign that electricity had even been invented. Only miles of dark, empty fields lay around us, the smell of manure plugging our nostrils.

In the gathering darkness, my brother and I nestled against the shiny leather seats of my father's new '65 red Rambler, as, swearing under his breath, he stopped and once again consulted another of the half dozen maps he kept in his glove compartment. Where do you think we are, I wanted to ask, but I knew better. We were not allowed to talk to my father when he was lost. My mother held her head rigid in the front seat, ready to flash me a silencing look if I dared make a peep. But I didn't, partly out of habit, but also because I was spellbound—in love with being lost. Countries in Europe were so small, a quarter of the size of most provinces in Canada, so that within a half hour's drive we could be in a whole new land.

But which one? Belgium? Austria? Perhaps we had ventured even farther afield, even dangerously so, and were approaching a Communist country. *Russia!*

Steeped in unknown surroundings I wasn't allowed to

ask about, the landscape revealed itself. In the middle of a flat, muddy field, I spotted what appeared to be two ploughed mounds of earth, but I knew they were a farming couple. At ten, I had developed an eye for the subtle national differences between farmers. Germans were the friendliest, often waving when they saw the Canadian sticker beside our license plate, while the French flat out ignored us.

But this couple seemed different, more suspicious, furtive. Pointedly pretending they didn't see the Rambler with the lost Canadian family, they crouched lower, like lumpen mounds about to sink back into the earth. Did they think we were spies? Or were they old people, still mired in memories of the war, feigning invisibility as an enduring habit? We drove past them again and again, in mesmerizing circles, and I was almost disappointed when my father shouted with relief as he finally spotted a sign, and bulleted back to the Autobahn.

* * *

The day I found myself lost—truly lost, I had wanted to get home quickly. I had been at my swimming lesson on the base, and had seen a thick fog rolling in from the day's drizzle. Ordinarily I would have taken my usual route, a picturesque country road that curved past the PMQ's and a stretch of the Black Forest before turning toward Hugelsheim, the church steeple reassuringly announcing the town's presence. But this particular route—a new paved road linking the base and town that my father drove back and forth to work everyday—was more direct, a 20-minute walk at most.

A ten-year-old girl walking alone is a relic from another time. But back then, it never occurred to me that I could be harmed. "Watch out for airmen," my mother would sometimes warn me when I went out alone on my bike, but in those days when "sex"—let alone "pedophile" or "rapist"— weren't part of a ten-year-old's vocabulary, she had never offered a clear explanation as to the nature of these threats. I assumed it had something to do with the pejorative tone my father always used in referring to men without rank. Usually single, and living in barracks, these were the men who were out of shape and had Coke and doughnuts ("*just white flour and sugar!*") on their coffee breaks. Whenever we passed such a man on the base, invariably short and pudgy, without the smart corporal's stripe on his uniform, my father would sneer: "*Doughnut eater!*" It was the most scathing insult he had for a man. So why would I need to be afraid of them?

Besides, on that foggy day, walking on a grassy footpath that ran alongside the road, I had other worries: a surprisingly disappointing swimming lesson. Apparently I hadn't mastered the front crawl, and wasn't going to advance from Juniors into Intermediates. My kick was off, too splashy and uncoordinated with my arms, no matter how hard I tried. "Naw, you still didn't get it right," my father had said the one time he had come to watch me, and I was grateful that he hadn't seen me today. All that healthy eating, and look at me! I felt the weight of his disgust and how my failure to achieve this thing I had tried to master—a first for me at ten—would give me nothing to talk about at dinner. For our mealtime conversations generally took one of two forms: my father pontificating on some new health theory, railing against the doughnut eaters, or my brother and I reporting on something we had done well. Otherwise we remained silent.

The ground was slippery, with scraggly, wet grass that was hard to walk on. I was wearing a sleeveless, white fitted blouse and a pair of pink pedal pushers that had become tight around my hips, due to the fact that I was "developing into a young woman" as my mother noted. My still wet chlorine-scented ponytail was clamped to the back of my neck, my bathing suit rolled into a damp towel under one arm. I kept my eyes on the ground to avoid the puddling parts of grass. Another failure as, within minutes, the toes and canvas sides of my runners were completely sodden.

After five minutes or so, I looked up, expecting to see the church spire of Hugelsheim in the distance. Instead, I found myself heading into a denser bank of fog, this one weirdly lit from within by a harsh, leeching light. The road ahead was barely visible, a smudge, which created a disorienting sensation, as if I would disperse and become unseen as well. I concentrated on staying on the grassy path, because I didn't want to get hit by a car. After what seemed a very long time, the illuminated whiteness thinned, and I could make out the road again.

But still, no church spire. Just a long stretch of fields and the grass path ahead. Grass that I was beginning to see —now that I was focused on it so intently—wasn't trampled down by other footprints, and looked as if it had been rarely used.

The harsh hum of an engine flared up behind me, then became more muted—the car was slowing down.

My chest tightened. A new female knowledge seeped

inside me. I didn't have to worry about being hit by a car. I had been *seen*. And I had been since I was a tiny smudge in the distance, a lone girl on a road few people walked on. It was a *him* in the car. I knew this because of the way he had slowed down to watch me. A car holding a nice family would go faster because they wanted to get out of the miserable weather and rush towards the warmth of their house. This man had no particular place to go, and was appraising me.

Keep walking, I told myself. Do not run. Do not look back. Make sure you look like you know where you're going. Any minute now, the church spire will appear like a re-proachful parental finger rising in the sky, saying: Where were you? What took you so long?

But only more fog lay ahead, changing as if alive—light to dark, with an unnerving boxlike solidity to it, as if I were walking through a compound of empty rooms. Without turning, I sensed that the car was about five feet behind me now. Four. Within seconds, its headlights would be nosing my elbow. My sense of distance and timing was thrown off, but I now had a new sense of another's timing: how long it would take to stop, grab, and do whatever it was that men could do to young girls.

My runners were now completely soaked, my shirt clamped to my back, making me feel like a wet paper bag. Disposable. Like something that could be crumpled up and thrown away. Why weren't other cars coming from Hugelsheim? With warm, golden headlights, a familiar face that might recognize me? Or a hay wagon, driven by a kindly old German couple?

Or, my father?

For the first time in my life, I felt an inversion of things.

My home life was deeply abnormal. Why was I out here alone? Even if we had a phone, there was no way I could phone my father and ask him to pick me up. And I knew with a sharp, sudden pang, that the man in this car must know this too. That I was not just a girl, but a disposable girl, one who was cold and wet in the fog for a definite reason. My father didn't love me enough to give me a ride home—an unsettling realization to have at the best of times, and even more so out here. This man would know that I had done something wrong—or at least not right enough to deserve my father's care. He would know that a red Rambler wasn't going to come tearing out from the direction of Hugelsheim, screeching to a halt in front of me, with a man who looked like a trophy jumping out to say: "For God's sake, get in!"

An ache—a longing for something as simple as the warmth of a car seat and a caring male presence—rose up in me, as the man pulled up. I suppressed it. He drove slowly, keeping pace. Then he drove off, the hiss of his car dissolving into a welcome silence.

Two more cars pulled up alongside me in this way, paused, looked, then left.

I had been walking for what felt like at least a half an hour now, maybe more. My neck hurt from holding my head down, but I couldn't chance looking up, to face the growing dread of the illusive church steeple. How much longer did I have to walk before the grass turned to cobblestones under my feet? How much longer could I trick myself into thinking I had merely miscalculated the distance?

A particularly high patch of thistles scraped my ankles, adding insult to the indignity of soaked feet. Then I stopped cold, recalling something my father had once said. We were had been driving to the nearby city of Rastatt, and he had commented on the new paved roads that were being built, so new that they weren't even on the maps yet.

"Will you look at that!" he had said. "Will you just look at that! That road wasn't even built a month ago!" For the first time since I had set out from the base, I raised my head and looked thoroughly at the landscape around me. Only dark, muddy fields stretching out on either side, walled by white fog banks. Could I have taken the wrong road? Was there another road leading out from the base that I wasn't aware of? One that, in my haste to get home and, with my naturally poor sense of direction, I could have taken by mistake?

Think, I told myself. Retrace your steps. You were at the base, you saw the fog rolling in, you wound your towel more tightly around your bathing suit, you barrelled off at the checkpoint station. Did you see two roads?

Being lost had always been an adventure for me, those family excursions on unknown roads that could lead any-where. Now, with rising panic, I considered that I could have headed east instead of west. I could be miles away from Hugelsheim. *Miles.*

My legs were so tired I could barely stand. If I could just sit down for a few minutes, I could figure out what to do next. Turning around and going back to the base seemed to be the next logical step, but I needed something, a rock to sit on. That round black shape across the road. Was it a mound of dirt, or a boulder?

The hiss coming from the distance was barely audible at first, but it needled up my spine. This time I turned around to look at the car emerging from the whited-out horizon. Blurry, match-boxed-sized, it was moving slowly, too slowly, with an odd, pulsating brightness to its headlights. The light created two spangled whorls of colour, so the car lit looked like a float in a parade, hovering above the road in a kind of celebratory excitement.

I looked away. *This* was the airman my mother had warned me about. The one whose habits I suddenly, instinctively knew, just as I was understanding too much about men that day, one sickening realization after another volleying in. This man had no friends. He had been lying about in the barracks, bored. Then he decided to go out for a drive in this miserable weather because it was better than doing nothing. This was the airman who wanted to do me harm.

Hide, I told myself. But where? Had I missed anything when I looked around me? A house, a patch of forest, farmers? Surely if I squinted hard enough, I'd see a mound of earth that was really a nice German couple toiling out in those dark fields. The utter flatness of the fields, the absolute lack of shelter, made me want to cry.

And now the fog was clearing into a thin mist, making me more visible. With nothing else to do, I resumed walking, those exuberantly spangled headlights boring into my back. Being followed by him felt different than being followed by the others, because I could sense now that there was concern in the way those men had cautiously inched towards me—they had cared. This airman was taking his sweet time to prolong the excitement of watching me: two gangly legs jerking from developing hips, wet feet slipping on uneven clumps of grass. There was no point in keeping my head down because I knew I was on the wrong road. And he knew that I knew I was lost.

Tears sprang to my eyes, along with the bitterness of a new, sharp personal failure. This was the bleak, debilitating fear of being a lone female, and I suddenly hated this man for making me feel ordinary.

Thankfully I had no concept of sex, nor had I ever read any newspaper headlines about bodies being dismembered. I assumed that I would be tossed to the ground, he would throw himself on top of me, and it might hurt.

My walk was all wrong now, on the point of giving up. When he was a few feet away, I abruptly stopped, not just from exhaustion, as much as the need to get whatever was going to happen to me over with. Likely surprised, he pulled up to the side of the road, and after a few seconds, opened the passenger door and leaned out.

We looked at each other. He was moon-faced, with a fleshy chin nestling on rounded shoulders and small, dark eyes. Eyes that changed before me, something deeply restrained leaping out, a trembling eagerness acutely naked in its longing.

My shoulders jerked up in contempt. *A doughnut eater!* Even without seeing the rest of his body leaning towards me, I could tell it would be soft and pudgy from eating white flour and sugar, and I could sense his incomprehensible lack of self-disgust in that. His lips twitched up in a little smile as if he actually thought I would get in the car with him. I turned my head sideways, and saw, rising out of the mist, not more than a 100 metres away, the church steeple of Hugelsheim.

A few months later, my mother heard rumours of a "bad airman" and wouldn't let me go out alone for a while. Was it this man? I don't know but, if so, it was pride in my father that saved me. Fear of men became ingrained in my psyche that day, but contempt for those who were not of my father's calibre occupied a higher plane.

The man saw it too. My scorn, my unexpected disdain, made him duck his head back into his car and, in that instant, I took off. Running now, a gazelle, strength returned from the sheer exhilaration of knowing that someone like him would never catch up with the likes of me, thrilling as my feet hit the first cobblestone of the town's street, my father's daughter.

Acknowledgements

"Doughnut Eaters" won first prize in *PRISM international's* 2015 Non-Fiction Contest, and was published in their Spring 2015 issue.

"Prey" was published in *The Dalhousie Review*, Autumn 2013.

"The Girl Next Door" was published in *The Dalhousie Review*, Summer 2011.

"Shadow Selves" was published in *Other Voices*, Fall 2008.

"Thick" was published in *IMAGE,* Ireland's leading fashion magazine in February 2000.

"Valentine" was published in *IMAGE,* Ireland's leading fashion magazine in April 1999, and subsequently re-published in Great Britain's *You* magazine in February 2000, and in *TickleAce*, Fall 2000.

"Lord of the Manor" was published in *Other Voices* in Summer 1999.

"New Ground" was published in *The Antigonish Review* in Spring 1996.

About The Author

Diane Bracuk was born in Montreal, Quebec into a military family. She grew up on armed forces bases in Canada and Germany. She has a degree in English Literature from the University of Alberta. Her first short story "New Ground" was published in *The Antigonish Review* in 1996, and her story "Doughnut Eaters" won first place in *PRISM international's* 2015 Creative Non-Fiction contest. She lives in Toronto.

Printed in November 2015
by Gauvin Press,
Gatineau, Québec